THE SMOKING NUN

BOOK 4 NUN OF YOUR BUSINESS MYSTERIES

DAKOTA CASSIDY

The Smoking Nun (Book 4 Nun of Your Business Mysteries)

Copyright © 2019 by Dakota Cassidy

ISBN: 9781094951195

Imprint: Independently published

❀ Created with Vellum

ACKNOWLEDGMENTS

Welcome to the Nun of Your Business Mysteries! I so hope you'll enjoy the fourth adventure for Trixie Lavender and her pal, Coop, an ex-nun and a demon, respectively, trying to make their way in the world—*together*.

Please note, I currently live in the beautiful state of Oregon, just outside of Portland. And though not a native (New Yorker here!), I've fallen in love over and over again with my new home state every day for the five years we've been here. That said, I've created a district (sort of like the Pearl District, for you natives) in a suburb of Portland that is totally fictional, called Cobbler Cove.

You may recognize some of the places/streets/eateries I mention because they *do* exist, but keep in mind, I'm also flagrantly instituting my artistic license with the geography of gorgeous Portland to suit my own selfish needs. Some names for characters or groups/eateries/streets mentioned herein are completely fictitious.

As I've mentioned in my previous cozy mysteries, there's an ongoing mystery surrounding Coop and Trixie that will play out over the course of the series (sorrysorrysorry!), but the central mystery in each story will be all wrapped up in a pretty package with a nice bow by book's end.

That out of the way, welcome to the crazy world Trixie and Coop inhabit. I hope you come to love them as much as I do!

THE SMOKING NUN

CHAPTER 1

"Sister Ophelia, lovely day, isn't it?" I asked as I poked my head around the alleyway's corner at Our Lady of Perpetual Grace, dragging a bag of garbage to the dumpster where she stood.

The scent of cigarette smoke wended its way to my nostrils on this unusually lovely pre-spring day. Typically at this time of year in Cobbler Cove, we were still having fits and starts of colder weather that couldn't make up its mind what it wanted to do.

But today was the exception, and quite lovely indeed. The trees were standing at attention under the warm sun, hopeful buds on their limbs, the grass along the sidewalks was greening up, and there were people milling about in nothing more than light sweaters.

I lobbed the bag upward to drop it into the bin as one of my favorite nuns at Our Lady threw a half-smoked cigarette down on the ground, lifting her skirts and stomping it out with her ballet flats.

Her cheerful, wrinkled face poked out from her habit,

riddled with guilt as she huffed a sigh. She held up a petite hand in mock surrender.

"You caught me, child, and before you say anything, I know they're bad for me. I know it's a poor example for the children I teach at the school, but sometimes, in times of great stress, I just can't seem to kick the habit in its keister."

I smiled and winked at her, holding out my arm for her to take. "You know, I've heard it said it's harder to quit smoking than it is to quit drugs. Can you believe that? So with those words of wisdom, I cast absolutely no judgment here."

Sister O gave a light chuckle, the sound tinkling on the early afternoon breeze as she curled her knobby fingers around my forearm.

"That's ever so true, child. It could be crack I'm smoking, I suppose. Things could always be much worse."

I giggled as we made our way out of the alley to the long line of steps leading up to the magnificent walnut-stained doors of the church. I still got a small thrill when I saw the doors to a house of worship, despite my disenchantment with the church and its politics.

In my heart of hearts, these doors still led to hope, forgiveness, and redemption. All things everyone needs in this life from time to time, and for me, personally, they still brought a true sense of peace when I entered.

I looked up at the blue sky, puffy with white cotton-candy clouds, and smiled at the feel of the sun on my face, regretting the fact that most of the volunteer work I was doing today was indoors.

"So, are you ready for the speed-dating fundraiser tonight, Sister Ophelia? I've been here all afternoon setting up chairs and tables, and we had tons of people register. It looks like it's going to be a great turnout."

Our Lady of Perpetual Grace was hosting a fundraiser for the youth group's trip to a village in Africa (as crazy as it sounds to have an adult dating event help fund a *youth* group event) and me, Coop, and Higgs had been busily setting up the basement all day long in anticipation.

"I think the question is, are *you* ready, m'dear?" she crowed in her lilting voice, her smile teasing and light as she patted my arm and inhaled a deep breath of the fresh air.

I frowned momentarily and cocked my head. "Me? Aw, heck no. I'm not going to participate in the speed dating. I'm on punch duty."

Talking to strange men with the intent of having anything interesting to say while I twirled my hair and batted my eyelashes? No, thank you. I've never dated except for a little in high school, and I've certainly never been very good at flirting.

Plus, my life is so complicated right now—too complicated for casual dinners and movies. I had a demon inside me I needed to expel. That took precedence over keeping up the task of waxing my legs and dying my roots.

Sister Ophelia reached up and tugged a length of my hair, which, by the way, I'd been growing out and now was well past my collarbone.

"A pity. I'd bet a looker like you would have a full dance card by the end of the night."

Sister Ophelia knew most everything about my jaded past. From my hasty departure from Saint Aloysius By The Sea—minus the details about my demon, of course—to my faltering faith.

I'd met her when we'd volunteered to do some neighborhood community service, and both Coop and I liked her almost immediately. We shared a love of crime dramas (her particular favorite was repeats of *Unsolved Mysteries*) and mystery shows, and it didn't hurt that she was funny and quick-witted and the first to offer you a hug when you'd had a bad day.

She didn't seem to mind that I'd left the convent. She hadn't even pried when I didn't give her an explanation for leaving.

She'd simply said whatever my reasons, it was clear my heart was in the right place. And that, coming from someone I not only respected, but someone from my former sisterhood, warmed me to my core. We'd been friends of sorts ever since.

Something else to note, during the course of our budding friendship, one I'd entered hesitantly because she was, after all, blessed by the holy spirit and a vessel for the spiritual world. Sister Ophelia hadn't once sensed the demon in me...

Not once.

A relief? Sure. That enabled me to be close to the people I'd once treasured above all else. But didn't it also mean all the hoopla in the Good Book about nuns and priests sensing evil wasn't really true?

I don't know. I *do* know, it's one more bit of evidence to add to the pile of my rocked beliefs that I've packed away to address at another time.

"So, lovely girl? Are you going to dabble a little in the dating pool, maybe get your feet wet?" she asked, her bright eyes amused.

I grinned at her and drove my hands into the pockets of my jeans. "For now, I'm going to leave the dating to the experts like Miss Carla. She has the dating thing on lockdown."

Miss Carla Ratagucci could find a date at a monk convention, and that's not a fib. She had this charisma, this…this something that made men flock to her like a medium-rare rib eye.

Sister Ophelia frowned in clear disapproval, folding her hands together in a fist. "Miss Carla has many things, my child. Middle age and cankles are but two. Shall I go on?" she asked dryly.

I fought an unladylike snort. It wasn't kind to gossip, but what Sister Ophelia said was partially true. Miss Carla was definitely middle-aged and she definitely dressed in a manner that had created controversy every Sunday since I'd begun attending services a couple of months ago.

You always knew when Miss Carla entered and took a spot in one of the pews due to the ripple of sound from the other parishioners.

And yes, I've been attending Sunday services here and there. Oddly, the demon in me hasn't rejected the idea of my entering sacred ground. Though, I will tell you, I held my darn breath the first time I strolled inside to meet Higgs for lunch and he introduced me to his good friend, Father Rico.

That I didn't burst into flames when I shook his hand was a good sign. A good sign indeed. That Coop didn't either? The best sign ever, because ironically, my Coop loved the church and all the people in it. So far, she'd debunked every myth about demons I'd ever been taught.

Anyway, I liked Carla's free spirit, her confidence, and her colorful choice of clothing and makeup. She lived her life the way she wanted to and she didn't care what anyone said about it.

Which was a good thing, because *everyone* said something about it. She'd been dubbed Our Lady's personal maneater—always on the hunt for the next kill—a catty parishioner's words, not mine.

However, she's the one who'd come up with the idea of the speed-dating event and had somehow gotten it past Father Rico with his full approval. There was something to be said for the magic of Miss Carla.

I popped my lips. "You know you love Carla, Sister O."

She put her hands in front of her and chuckled, her eyes expressing her fondness. "That I do, but a spade's a spade, don't you agree, Trixie?"

"Well, before we judge Miss Carla, we should remember she's the one who came up with this speed-dating idea in the first place, and it's brought in a ton of money for the youth group. If no one's check bounces, all thirty of those children will be able to go to Africa and actually eat while they're there. You can't dispute that."

Sister Ophelia let out an exasperated sigh and arched a gray eyebrow. "You know how she did that, don't you?"

"How?"

"She invited all her jilted lovers, that's how. That'll fill up an entire convention center."

I had to hide my laughter as I encouraged her up the stairs, ignoring her stab at Carla's fickle ways. Yes, Carla was a serial dater, but why settle when you didn't have to?

"Now, now, Sister Ophelia. What does the scripture say

about pettiness and gossip?" I chided playfully.

"It says beware of a wolf in sheep's clothing, and Miss Carla's picture is right beneath."

I rolled my eyes at her when we reached the top of the steps, pulling open the heavy doors to allow her to enter first. "She's not a wolf, Sister O. Maybe a cougar, but certainly not a wolf."

Sister Ophelia's pixie-like laughter tinkled throughout the entryway to the church as we made our way toward the basement steps, leaving me smiling.

~

"*W*ow, what a turnout!" Higgs said with a whistle as we pushed our way through the throng of people who'd gathered for the big event, waving to Goose and Knuckles, who'd cleaned up just fine for tonight.

The basement was jam-packed with people, standing under the Edison lights we'd strung from the ceiling earlier today. High, round tables sat in clusters so the speed daters could move from place to place with ease.

There was a long table covered from one end to the other with all manner of snack foods and small hors d'oeuvres donated by the local restaurants to keep the daters from getting hangry.

I nodded as Higgs grabbed my hand to help navigate our way through the crowd. "It's all due to Miss Carla's magic."

He pulled me toward the punch table, where my duty as server awaited. "Is it just me or do you find it ironic that *speed dating* is going to fund a *youth* group's trip to Africa?"

"Do you know, before I stuck my nose in the middle of everything, what the title of this event was originally?"

Higgs gave me a skeptical glance. "I'm afraid to ask."

I giggled at the memory and breathed another sigh of relief that I'd been able to talk Carla out of it before the flyers went to the printer.

"Speed Dating For Christ's Sake—and there was a comma *after* the word dating."

I watched him visualize that sentence in his mind, and then he chuckled. "Hoo boy."

I grinned up into his handsome face—a face I liked more every day I spent with him. "Exactly. But better still? I talked her out of an auction for a date with the eligible men around town. Because I'm here to tell you, that idea was bandied about—and *you* were number one on her hit list, pal."

Higgs's dark eyes sparkled when he laughed and pounded his chest with his broad fist. "Did you take one for the team, Sister Trixie Lavender?"

I shook a warning finger at him. "I'm tellin' ya. It took some mighty fancy footwork on my part to talk her out of it, too. The kind that surely requires payback in the way of a dinner on you, kind sir."

"So I owe you a salad?" he teased, referring to our ongoing joke about how unhealthy his eating habits were.

I narrowed my eyes playfully at him and flicked the collar of his eggplant-purple dress shirt. "You know, the youth group is going to need funding for their ski trip in December. An auction could still happen if you're not careful."

Higgs held up his hands and backed away. "I surrender,"

he said, his gravelly voice pleasant in my ears. "Now, have I told you how pretty you look tonight, Miss Lavender?"

My face went up in flames then. My cheeks burned and my toes curled. I was wearing a dress, one Coop had helped me pick out. I loved the feminine pink and white floral print made out of a soft rayon material. It made me feel girly as the ruffles across the hem fluttered around my knees.

I also had on some soft pink heels; modest heels, mind you, and a little mascara and lip gloss, if you must know.

Okay, so I wanted to look pretty, but running the tattoo shop kept me in jeans and T-shirts most of the time. It was fun to dress up once in a while.

Or at least that's what I told myself as I'd blown out my hair and Coop had made some magic with her curling iron to give me soft curls around my face.

I curtsied to cover my embarrassment and spread the floaty skirt of my dress with my hand. "Thank you, Higgs. I *feel* pretty."

Out of the corner of my eye—because I always had trouble meeting Higgs's gaze when he complimented me—I happened to catch a glimpse of Sister Ophelia by the corner of the room where the bathrooms were located, her face flushed, and I wondered if she'd gone outside to have another one of her forbidden smokes.

Which reminded me, she'd mentioned being stressed, and I hadn't had the forethought to ask her what was troubling her until I was getting ready this evening. I made a note to myself to find her later tonight and check-in.

"Trixie!" I heard someone call out my name just as I

caught a glimpse of Higgs blanching at the sound of a familiar sultry voice. "Trixie!"

I turned to find Carla Ratagucci waving at me, her tight-fitting red and black color-block dress hugging her ample curves—which explained Higgs's reaction. Carla liked Higgs, and she made sure he knew it because she flirted with him every chance she had. Judging by the way she slinked toward us with a seductive sashay, she had no plans to stop flirting today.

"Don't you look gorge?" she cooed at me from a pair of full, very red lips as she grabbed my hand and twirled me around. Her signature perfume, a heavier musky scent, wafted under my nose as I spun.

I chuckled at her compliment and waved a hand up and down along her very bodacious length. "Forget me, would you look at you! I love your dress, and I'll never understand how you walk in those shoes, but I sure wish I could manage it because they make your legs look fantastic." I pointed to her stilettos with a shake of my head in admiration.

Carla flapped her hands at me and tucked one of her shoulder-length, inky-black curls behind her ear with a flirty smile. "These are nothing. You should have seen me back in the day. No heel or hairdo was too high for this girl." Then she gave Higgs a coy look and a smoldering gaze.

Higgs ran a finger around the edge of the collar of his shirt and swallowed, and I have to admit, I got a little kick out of seeing such a big, confidant man fall to pieces around the sexier-than-sin Carla.

But I decided to save him from her because that's what

friends do. I knew her suggestive language and constant flirting made Higgs feel uncomfortable.

I slipped my arm through hers and began to walk her away from my favorite ex-cop, who I'd swear hissed a sigh of relief.

"Have I mentioned what an amazing job you did, pulling this all together, Carla? I mean, this is really something. Just look at what you've done." I pointed to the packed room for effect.

She patted my arm and let out a huff. "All for the kids. Now, do you have a speed-dating card?"

"Me? Um, no. I'm running the punch table." And that was absolutely that.

But Carla shook her head and began to tug me toward a table with an infectious giggle. As we whizzed across the room, I waved to Deacon Delacorte, the newest addition to Our Lady fresh from, of all places, a peace mission in China.

Deacon Delacorte was a handsome, dark-haired man in his early forties with a frame like a pro wrestler and the face of an angel. I also waved to Deacon Cameron, an older gentleman with a head full of graying hair and an acne-scarred face. Both were still dressed in their afternoon mass attire, enjoying a cup of punch—the punch I should be serving them.

As we whisked past the punch, I pointed to the refresh-ment table before we came to a halt.

"Forget the punch, Trix. People can get their own punch —a monkey could get their own punch. You need a date, young lady. You're too pretty to be dateless, and after tonight, I bet you won't be for long." She patted the table where the index cards to write little notes about each participant sat stacked next to a cup of pencils. "Grab a pencil, honey."

I began to heartily protest, pressing my palms against the edge of the table to resist. "But—"

"But nothing!" she teased breathlessly with a wink of her artfully made-up smoky eye. "You do see there are more men than women, don't you?"

My eyes made a cursory sweep around the softly lit room, and I realized she was right. There were indeed more men than women.

I gulped and blanched at the same time. "But—"

"The children *need* you, Trixie! If we don't have enough women, the men will lose interest. C'mon. How can you say no to the children? If we don't keep these suckers here for as long as possible, they'll leave, and then where will the silent auction be? Dead and buried, that's where. We've gotten a lot of donations for the auction. It's money in the bag as long as we play this right. Now, we've got some fish on the line, we just need to reel 'em in!"

Blinking, I stared up at her. How was I supposed to defend myself against a plea like that? *Do it for the kids...*

Panic began to turn in my belly and my hands went cold and clammy. "But I...I don't know the first thing about dating. I can't—"

"But look, you're to-die-for, want-to-gouge-her-gorgeous-eyes-out friend Coop is helping, and as much as I want to hate her for being so maddeningly stunning, I can't because if *anyone* can get the men to stick around, she can."

Carla pointed over my shoulder two or three tables behind us where Coop, wide-eyed and flawless, sat like she'd just been dropped in the middle of the twentieth level of Hell.

Don't ask. Just know that level truly exists…then let that bit of information simmer on your back burner for a while like it has mine.

Oh, dear. Poor Coop. I knew Carla had likely bamboozled her. I mean, who could resist her sultry voice and breathy conviction when she wanted something? No one. That's who. Especially if she'd told her it was for the children, whom Coop absolutely adored.

And then there was Cal. Coop and Cal, the fellow Higgs had hired at the shelter, were a little bit smitten with one another in the sweetest, most innocent of ways. Over the last few months, they'd had coffee (or orange juice, for my Coop) and lunch together at least once a week.

There'd been a lot of questions from Coop about the funny feeling in her tummy every time she saw Cal, but we hadn't had "the talk" as of yet. Heck, I didn't know if we needed to have the talk. I didn't even know if I knew enough about the talk to have it in the first place.

I only knew, Coop didn't know any more about dating than I did. And I didn't want Cal to see her at a table and get his feelings hurt because she was caught up in something she didn't know how to say no to.

Carla spun me around and patted my shoulder with a wide grin, her white teeth gleaming, leaving me feeling like the prey to her wolf—which is how I imagine Higgs feels.

"Now, you just sit here and be pretty, Trix. They'll flock to you like moths to a flame. Trust me. *I know men.*"

And believe you me, I believed her.

As she coaxed me onto a high barstool and planted the

cards and a pencil in front of me, I began another weak protest. "But—"

"But nothing. Just be yourself, Trixie, and enjoy! And thanks for helping an old girl out," she breathed, tweaking my cheek seconds before I heard Father Rico, our host for tonight, tap the microphone to announce the beginning of the event.

His words all blended together in one big sound, like the noise the adults make on Charlie Brown. I was about to speed date—and I was terrified.

And suddenly, a very tall man with hawkish blue eyes and a tweed blazer over a black T-shirt was in front of me. He had a slope to his shoulders that made him look shorter than he actually was, but his smile reached his eyes well enough. He stuck out his slender, veined hand as I licked my lips in nervous panic.

"I'm Jason. You are?"

I'm thinking about killing Carla...

Shaking off my commandment-breaking thought, I cleared my throat and stuck my hand out, trying to be as confident as Carla. I could do this—for the kids.

"Trixie. Trixie Lavender. Nice to meet you."

He slid into the chair, his long legs encased in trousers with a meticulously sharp pleat down along the thigh, and unbuttoned his jacket.

"Nice to meet you, too, Trixie." There was a small, awkward pause as all my people skills flew right out the window, until Jason said, "Before we get started. Do you know where the crab legs are? My friend told me there'd be all-you-can-eat crab legs, but I can't find them anywhere."

"He lied."

14

The words shot from my lips before I could stop them, making me consider clapping my hand over my mouth to keep more from escaping.

Jason, who, if I'm honest, really did have terrific light brown hair, shiny and thick with these fascinating caramel highlights, made a distasteful face.

"There's a sucker born every minute, huh?" he joked with a brief smile.

"Well, if you believed there'd be crab legs at a speed dating event, held in a church, of all places, then yes. There's a sucker born every minute," I confirmed.

He threw his head back and laughed, all that shiny hair bouncing with its incredible volume. "You're a comic."

"No. I'm an ex-nun."

Jason blinked, the fringe of his lashes sweeping his cheeks. *"Really?"*

Oh, heavens. It was as though I couldn't stop myself from playing the honesty card.

"I think we've established I'm anything but untruthful," I responded, and then I smiled uneasily, hoping to soften my words.

The moment I thought we were simply going to sit in awkward silence due to Jason's shock, the bell rang and he was up and virtually running off to the next table.

On a sigh, as the participants shuffled, I took a sneak peek behind me to see Coop deeply ensconced in conversation with a very attractive man, then throwing her head back and doing her strange imitation of a laugh à la her idol, Alexis Carrington. All the while, a line of men waited with impatient yet hopeful looks on their faces.

Maybe I should take a cue from my demon friend and

act my way through this.

"Hello," whispered a pensive young man, maybe no more than thirty.

Squaring my shoulders, I smiled at him in his baggy tan shorts, flip-flops and a faded tie-dyed tunic, settling in to act my way out of this.

"Hi. I'm Trixie. Nice to meet you."

"Jeremiah," was all he offered, before taking his seat and tucking his long, scraggly blond hair behind his ears. Then he placed his elbows on the table, cupped his chin in his hands and stared at me.

But he didn't just stare at me, he stared at me with such intensity, squinting his eyes, it was as though he was looking for my soul.

I fidgeted in my chair, twisting a length of my hair around my finger, which I suppose could have been interpreted as flirty but was really out of nervousness.

"Um—"

"Shhh!" he whisper-yelled, flashing a ruddy, tanned hand up in front of my mouth. "Don't talk, dude."

I leaned back to avoid his touch and cocked my head. "*Excuse me?*"

Was dating always this rude, *dude*?

Jeremiah shook a calloused finger at me with an intense gaze. "Just stay still. *Please*. I like to sit for a sec and get a feel for your aura, ya know? Really get into your core and dig around so I can *feeeeel* your soul. I can't do that if you're making noise."

I blinked, and as he dug around in my core, I doodled him a note in big block letters on my index card while I patiently waited for him to finish *feeeeeling* my soul.

When he finally spoke, his serious gaze turned suddenly fun and friendly as he reached across the table to grab my hand. Apparently, my soul met with his soul's approval.

"So, heeey. S'up?" He grinned. A very pleasant grin, I might add.

But I'd been soured, and no amount of smiling and dude-ing me were going to change that.

So I looked at him for a long moment before I held up the index card in front of my face and let him read what I'd wrote.

Not if my soul and your soul were the last souls on Earth, DUDE. And then I tacked on a smiley emoji for good measure.

I was saved Jeremiah's reaction when there was a piercing scream as the crowd rippled and moved, drawing my eye to Deacon Delacorte's tall figure at the corner of the basement by the exit door.

And then I heard him yell in his raspy voice, "Someone call 9-1-1! Sister Ophelia needs help!"

I jumped out of my chair and began elbowing my way through the crowd toward Sister Ophelia, my heart clamoring in my chest.

My first thought was she'd had a heart attack; she *is* in her seventies. But after pushing my way through the throngs of people to get to her, I came to a screeching halt at the wide-open exit door, where I saw Deacon Delacorte shaking his head, hair glistening with droplets of water, a deep sorrow in his eyes.

"She's...she's gone!" he wailed mournfully, falling to his knees with Sister Ophelia in his arms. "Gone!"

CHAPTER 2

*A*s I dropped to my knees on the floor beside him, Deacon Delacorte held my favorite nun under her arms, as though he'd dragged her in from outside, and sobbed, letting his chin fall to his chest.

Her head leaned in crooked fashion to the left side of his wide chest, pressed against his stole, her body crumpled and twisted in an odd position on the floor, and her wimple was missing. She'd had her wimple on when I'd seen her earlier this evening.

I reached out a shaky hand to circle her wrist, and indeed, Sister Ophelia had no pulse. Her skin was a bit clammy and definitely a little wet, leading me to believe Deacon Delacorte had definitely found her outside.

And that was when I saw her neck. An ugly blue and purple ring stained her wrinkled skin, and her gray-blue eyes bulged outward, leaving me to fight to keep from hissing my horror.

My stomach heaved at the ligature mark, but I pressed my trembling fingers to her wrist, closed my eyes and sent out a wish to the universe for her safe passage. I wanted to scoop her up in my arms and cling to her, but I knew in my gut foul play had played a part in this, and I didn't want to contaminate any possible evidence.

"Trixie Lavender?" I heard Coop call as she, too, dropped to her knees, placing a hand on my shoulder. "*Oh, no, no, no. Not Sister Ophelia,*" she said, her voice tight and stiff, which is as close to emotion as she can get.

But emotion is what got the better of me then, and instead of making sure the police were on their way, I caved, leaning against Coop as my eyes welled with tears and I began to sob.

She wrapped an arm around me and squeezed but let me go when Higgs approached and asked, "Coop? May I?"

As I felt Coop leave my side, Higgs wrapped me up in his big arms. I caught a flash of the intricate sleeve tattoos on his forearm before I allowed myself an indulgence. I buried my face in his wide chest and cried—cried so hard with such great, gulping sobs, I thought my throat would surely burst.

And he let me, running his wide palm over my back. As the initial hush of horror wore off and people milled about and Coop managed to get Deacon Delacorte to let Sister Ophelia's body go, Higgs rocked back and forth on his feet, solid, steady, and reassuring.

The scent of him and his cologne filled my nose, woodsy and musky. In that moment, I realized how safe I felt with him. How protected.

It was only when I heard the police arrive that I knew I had to gather myself for Sister Ophelia's sake. She wouldn't want me in hysterics when this was clearly a case of foul play. I didn't doubt that for a second. The marks around her neck were more than enough proof for me. I didn't need forensics to confirm that, and as a fellow amateur crime solver and lover of mysteries, Sister Ophelia wouldn't want me blubbering all over the place. She'd want me to get my head in the game.

Wiping my eyes with a fist, I leaned back away from Higgs's tall frame and brushed at his purple shirt, covered in my tears and mascara, which was definitely not waterproof as advertised.

"I'm sorry," I whispered, reaching up and cupping his jaw for a brief moment before I muttered my thanks and turned to wipe the remainder of my tears and compose myself as the police rushed in.

Detective Tansy was the first to find me, reaching out a hand, her sharp blue eyes full of sympathy, her voice cracking. "Oh, Trixie, love. I'm so sorry."

Tansy knew how much I liked Sister Ophelia, and she knew how much I'd been enjoying attending services after such a long time away. Since the last case we'd worked on, involving some of the homeless men from Higgs's shelter, when she'd asked me to be a liaison of sorts for bereaved victims of crime, we'd spent a good deal of time together—both in working and social capacities.

There hadn't been a murder since the last maniac, Detective Griswald, had been on the loose and selling the organs of the homeless on the black market, but we'd ventured into several domestic disputes and the like together with great success.

My capacity as liaison was nothing official. I didn't receive a paycheck nor was I privy to many details in some cases, but it was my way of giving back to the community, and as hard as it was to find the right words of comfort for the family of someone with a gunshot wound or the victim of domestic violence, I never said no when Tansy called.

Thus far, I'd had no reason to poke my nose in where it didn't belong due to the nature of the cases we'd worked together. Since Detective Griswald's case, they'd all been pretty cut and dried.

Yet, this time was different. Sister Ophelia was my friend and a confidant in some respects, and someone had *hurt* my friend. Seeing her so broken made every square inch of me ache not just with sadness, but the need to find who'd done this.

Still, I squeezed Tansy's hand in return and shook my head, inhaling deeply. "Thanks, Tans."

"Do we know anything? Did you see anything, Trixie?"

"I didn't see anything and I don't know anything other than I'm certain she was murdered. *Certain.*"

Tansy's sympathy-filled eyes went from soft to hard in seconds. She pushed a hand through her short blonde hair and cocked her head. "Say again?"

"I *know* she was murdered, Tansy. You'll see when you get a glimpse of the bruises on her neck. It looks like she was strangled, but I got…too caught up in the emotion of it all when I saw her, and I…"

Tansy looked down at me, her eyes soft once more. She tucked my hair behind my ear and murmured, "Aw, Trixie, love. This one's too close, eh? How about you sit this one out?"

But I shook my head again, squaring my shoulders. "No. I can't. I think you know why I can't. Please, if nothing else,

DAKOTA CASSIDY

just let me shadow you, okay? Maybe I'll hear something or see something that can be helpful. I'll feel helpless if I don't do something."

She winked and nodded with a resigned sigh as she pulled her trusty notepad from the pocket of her navy blazer. "All right, but you remember our deal, Miss Marple. No interference with the crime scene. You may observe only. I speak to everyone first. Period." Then she pointed her finger over my shoulder at Higgs. "Bring the big galoot with you for support. This one won't be easy."

Higgs was behind me in a second, his warm hands resting on my shoulders. "Tansy's right. Let her do the work. You're too close to this one, Trixie."

I could only nod as the forensics team began to cordon off the area with yellow crime scene tape and Tansy talked with Deacon Delacorte, who was beside himself.

Goose and Knuckles found their way through the crowd and when they reached me, Knuckles held out his brawny arms. "Trixie girl. I'm sorry. Dang, I'm so sorry."

I flew into his warm embrace, pressing my face to his burly shoulder for only a second before I leaned back and couldn't help but ask, "Did you see anything, Knuckles?"

Goose put his thin hand on Knuckles's shoulder and shook his bandana-covered head. "We were over by the mini quiches when it went down, kiddo. We didn't see anything." He chucked me under the chin. "You okay? Want me to grab you something to wet your whistle?"

Sighing, I gave him a watery smile. "Thanks, Goose, but I'm okay. I'm more interested in what Deacon Delacorte saw. I mean, *who* would do such a thing? Who would hurt someone as kind and as funny as Sister Ophelia?"

"So you're sure someone hurt her? What makes you say that?" Knuckles asked with a frown, an eyebrow topped with three silver studs rising in question.

Shivering, I wrapped my arms around my waist, but my conviction hadn't wavered. "I have no doubt she was strangled. There were horrible bruise marks on her neck. It was…it was dreadful."

Goose whistled, driving his finger into the pockets of his best pair of jeans. "What a shame. I liked her a lot. She was a firecracker, that one. Always findin' a way to quote scripture to me. Even made a deal with me. She said if I came to one Sunday sermon, she'd get a tattoo. Can ya believe a nun with a tattoo?" He cackled at the memory. "She was a fine woman, Trixie. I'm sure sorry she's gone."

But I was no longer hearing what Goose was saying. Instead, I found myself listening to Deacon Delacorte and Deacon Cameron talk to Tansy and Oziah Meadows, or Oz, as we called him.

Deacon Delacorte looked positively shredded. His normally tanned skin was pale and his usually erect spine sagged.

"I only went outside to catch a breath of fresh air!" Deacon Delacorte cried out as he pressed his fingers to his mouth. "And…and…she was just there—on the ground—crumpled in a heap. So I ran and grabbed her because it was pouring and she was getting wet. I thought she'd collapsed, or maybe it was her heart, but…"

Deacon Cameron slapped him on the back. "Easy, Davis. There was nothing you could do."

Officer Meadows tipped his reddish-brown head in acknowledgement at me before he returned to scribbling on his pad while Tansy shot questions at Deacon Delacorte—whose first name was apparently Davis.

I didn't know the deacons' first names, and while a nun, I'd never addressed any by their given names. Thus, it sounded odd to hear him called Davis.

"So Mr. Delacorte, did you see Sister Ophelia go outside? Did you see her talk to anyone tonight? Did anything look off color to you? Out of sorts, maybe?" Tansy asked.

But Davis Delacorte shook his head with a rapid side-to-side motion. "Everything was fine as far as I knew. In fact, earlier today, we were in the business of getting to know one another—I'm new here, you see. And then we chatted about the lesson for Bible study she'd planned for next week's youth group. I helped her select the scripture."

The moment Tansy mentioned the words *out of sorts* was the moment I remembered our chat earlier today and, as per usual, despite my promise to her, I blurted, "Did she seem upset in any way, Deacon Delacorte? Stressed maybe?"

Davis looked surprised, his angelically handsome face paling further. "Stressed, Trixie? No. No-no. Not at all. She was in a good mood when I saw her this afternoon. As far as I knew, everything was fine."

Tansy hitched her jaw at me and leaned in toward my ear. I thought surely she was going to reprimand me for interfering, but instead she asked, "What makes you ask if Sister Ophelia was stressed?"

I guess now wasn't the time to keep secrets, but I internally apologized to Sister Ophelia anyway. This was for her own good.

"She was smoking. She said the only time she couldn't kick the habit was when she was stressed."

"Did you ask her *why* she was stressed?" Oz wondered, his deep voice soothing and calm.

Closing my eyes, I swallowed my regret and more tears. "I didn't. I should have, but I didn't. We got to talking about the speed-dating event and the conversation just got away from us, I guess."

Oh, I could kick myself for not remembering that until now when it was too late!

Oz scribbled some more on his pad as Father Rico approached. Short and stout, he waddled his way over to us and held out a hand to Higgs, giving him a pat before he held it out to me.

His soulful dark eyes, a rich coal black, searched mine. "Trixie, are you all right? I know you and Sister Ophelia had struck up quite a friendship. How can I help ease your pain?"

He was such a kind man. I'd liked him the instant Higgs had introduced us. His wise words and calm approach to my faltering faith had warmed me from the inside out.

I loved to listen to his rich baritone throughout the rectory when he gave his sermon. He didn't preach doom and destruction, sin and sorrow. Rather, his messages were always of hope and the gift of life, and I'd come to respect how he delivered the Word to his parishioners.

Gripping his pudgy, dimpled hand in return, I sought to soothe him. "She was a part of Our Lady long before I came along, Father. So the better question is, how are *you*?"

He grimaced, his eyes squinting, making the wrinkles around them deepen. "Sister Ophelia was a wonderful servant for the Lord. So vibrant and fun, but she took no guff. I don't know how Our Lady will manage without her. It's a terrible tragedy. She was so upset earlier, and I was so pressed for time with Carla breathing down my neck—"

"Upset?" I blurted, again forgetting my promise to Tansy. "About what?"

Father Rico's shoulders sagged beneath his casual black clerical shirt as he shook his head, his eyes full of grief. "I don't know, Trixie. She came to me earlier this evening and said it was imperative she speak to me, but we were about to begin the speed-dating event and I had announcements to make. So I put her off. Sister Patricia was with me at the time. She can attest to the fact that Sister Ophelia appeared...frazzled, I guess is the word I'd use."

Frazzled. When I'd seen her earlier, she'd been easy-breezy. So what had happened to her between the time I'd left her at the church doors until tonight?

Father Rico pointed over my shoulder. "Here's Sister Patricia now. Maybe she can help?"

Tansy held up a finger and a warning flashed in her eyes. "Let me handle this, love."

Sister Patricia, far more staid than Sister Ophelia, rushed toward us, her wimple floating behind her, her hands clenched together.

"Father Rico!" she cried, her birdlike eyes darting from face to face. "What happened?"

Tansy stepped between them and held up a hand. "You are?"

Her face went from worried to fearful as she fingered the cross around her neck. "Sister Patricia Latimer."

"All right then, Sister Patricia. Father Rico claims you

were with him when Sister Ophelia asked to speak with him on an urgent matter. Is that so?" Tansy asked, pen poised over her notepad.

Sister Patricia's normally pinched face crumbled as her thin fingers continued to worry her cross. "Yes," she whispered quietly. "She was very concerned about something tonight."

Tansy lifted her chin, her eyes assessing. "But I'm assuming you don't know why she fret?"

Sister Patricia's eyes darkened for a fraction of a second before she straightened her spine, her clear skin pale but for the two red spots on her cheeks. "I don't. No. But she appeared quite upset. She said it was urgent she speak to Father Rico about a concern she had."

As I listened to Sister Patricia tell Tansy what had passed, I stayed as quiet as I possibly could. Absorbing the words she spoke, watching the way she tried to remain calm, I couldn't help but feel an underlying current of nervous energy.

But I couldn't put my finger on why. Sister Patricia was a tough nut to crack. She was all about the rules, she spoke in the condescending manner one would expect from a crotchety, Bible-thumping nun from the days of old, even though she couldn't be more than forty. I often joked with Sister Ophelia that at any moment, I expected her to pull a ruler from her habit and whack someone over the knuckles.

But tonight, I was seeing a different Sister Patricia—a frightened one. The question was, why?

I lost my focus when I saw them put Sister Ophelia's body in a bag and load her onto a gurney, my eyes once more welling with tears as they zipped it up and carried her body off.

Higgs squeezed my shoulders for support. He'd remained mostly silent throughout the questioning of Father Rico and company, respecting Tansy's wishes, but I knew he'd want to talk about the events of the night as much as I'd need him to hear my thoughts on them, too.

He was often the person I confided in when I was blue after a particularly difficult call with Tansy, and I cherished his calm approach and wise reasoning.

It was when the forensics team came inside via the exit door, carrying a plastic bag containing evidence, that I gripped one of his hands, hard.

Sister Ophelia's wimple, clearly soaking wet but still in one piece, in one bag.

And in the other—a lone cigarette butt.

More proof Sister Ophelia had indeed been stressed.

CHAPTER 3

"*M*ornin', Trixie, darlin'. Did ya manage to get any sleep?" Livingston asked as I entered Inkerbelle's, his light Irish accent warm and soft.

Coop had scooped him up and brought him in for an early client, leaving me to attempt to sleep in, but to no avail. I don't think I slept a wink.

I reached out a hand and stroked his round head, marveling at his glassy green eyes as he perched on the beautiful handmade limb Knuckles had crafted for him.

"I didn't sleep. I tossed and turned."

"Aw, my sweet. I hate that you're goin' through this. Ya do know that, don't ya?"

Sighing, I chucked him under the chin and smiled, my eyes grainy and tired. "I do. I know you're not a fan of the church as a whole, but I appreciate your sympathies none-theless."

"Roight. I'm not a fan of anytin' havin' to do with the threat of the fiery depths, for sure. But I didn't wish the sister any ill for the preachin' she did about the glory of redemption. I rather liked Sister Ophelia, even if she was scared out of her wits about my very existence."

I laughed. Sister Ophelia had indeed been afraid of Livingston. The first time she'd come to the shop to bring me a flyer to hang on our community board for a bake sale, she'd nearly had a chicken when Livingston had ruffled his feathers.

She'd kept a safe distance from that moment on, explaining her fear of birds after being attacked by an overzealous parakeet as a child.

"Trixie," Coop called from the back of the shop, making her way toward me, her strut sleek as a panther's. "How are you this morning?"

"Tired. You?"

Coop gave me a long look, her green eyes dull in comparison to their normal shine. "I'm sad, too, Trixie Lavender. Sister Ophelia was a part of our community. Now, we've lost a part of our community. An important, special part."

I nodded sadly and inhaled a deep breath as I made my way behind the counter where the cash register sat. "We have."

Leaning on the counter, she tucked the long strands of her gorgeous auburn hair behind her ear. "So are we going to figure out who killed her?"

My lips lifted in a weak grin. That was my Coop. Ride or die. She knew I was beside myself about Sister Ophelia's death. She also knew I wouldn't rest until I found out who'd killed her even though I hadn't said a word.

Gnawing the inside of my cheek, I straightened our card

reader and tried to shake off the cobwebs and vestiges of my shock.

"We are. I promise. But first I think I just need to gather my head."

Coop frowned and tapped a finger on the counter. "You don't need to gather it. It's on your shoulders, right above your neck."

As tired as I was, I couldn't help but laugh at my demon and her literal take on everything. "Gathering my head means getting it together, Coop. I mean, I need to sort my thoughts. I think I'm still in shock is all. I haven't had time to think about anything but seeing Sister Ophelia lying there…"

I gulped and gripped the edge of the cool counter as a vision of her, pale and battered, flew through my mind's eye —it was the same one that had haunted me all night long and kept me from closing my eyes.

Clearly, I was overly emotional due to my lack of sleep, but that wouldn't get this crime solved. I needed to find my spine. Pronto.

"Are ya sure 'twas murder, Trixie? I know what ya said last night, but I wasn't sure if it was the ramblin' of your grief, or 'twere a credible retelling of the incident."

My eyes narrowed at the memory of Sister Ophelia's neck, and at Livingston, who occasionally liked to chalk things up to the hysterical woman theory. "Do you know anyone who dies by natural causes with ligature marks around their neck—marks so brutal, it left her skin blue and purple with bruises? I'm *positive* it was murder, Livingston. Positive as I stand here before you. Someone murdered her, and I'm not going to rest until I find out who."

He spread his beautiful gray and brown wings and shook them out. "Aw, don't get your knickers in a twist, Trixie. I'm just checkin'. I only want to help ya."

Coop tapped Livingston's beak with a fingernail. "You hush, Quigley Livingston. If Trixie says it was murder then it was murder. I saw Sister Ophelia, too, and in all my days, I've only seen one case with marks like the ones on her neck."

I shouldn't ask. I knew I'd regret asking. But I asked, "You've seen marks like that before?"

Coop stared back at me, her almost emotionless eyes intent when they captured mine. "Do I sense regret in your question?"

Rolling my eyes, I nodded. "Never mind. I don't want to know why you've seen ligature marks like that."

Coop bounced her head in agreement. "I thought not. So let's move on to something else." She pulled her phone from the pocket of her skinny jeans. "Look."

I took the phone from her and scrolled the pictures she'd taken last night. Several were selfies of the men she'd speed dated, all grinning like Cheshire cats, but some were of the actual event—and of Sister Ophelia's body.

"You took pictures?"

It was then she reached out a hand, one I'm pretty sure was meant to comfort me, and placed it on my shoulder. "I hope you won't find it disrespectful, but I, too, believe someone murdered Sister Ophelia, and that made my chest feel tight followed by an emotion I can't yet describe. Maybe it was anger. I'm still unclear. Humans have so many emotions, they confuse me with their inflating numbers." She paused as she pondered that, and then she said, "It doesn't matter. If we're going to find out who killed the sister, we have to be practical. Practicality means gathering evidence and pictures are evidence. I knew you'd want evidence, and I knew you'd want to investigate."

"Ahh, good on ya, Coop! Yer gettin' the hang of this human ting, you surely are," Livingston cooed approval.

As I scrolled the pictures, I nodded. "You sure are, Coop DeVille. Thanks for keeping your head on straight last night while I had a meltdown."

"My head is always on straight. I only know of one person whose head was on crooked, and that was after—"

"Coop!" both Livingston and I yelled in unison as I shook my finger at her in warning. "No tales from the hundredth level of Hell today."

"I'll have you know, there is no hundredth level. The levels only go as far as—"

"Coop!" we yelled again, but we all ended up chuckling together. A much-needed balm after last night's events.

At that point, Knuckles and Goose arrived for their morning clients, both quietly dropping a kiss on my forehead before heading off to their stations, and Coop went back to hers.

I can't tell you how grateful I am for these two men in my life—how grateful to have a purpose every day, a reason to get up. As I watched them settle into their chairs and gather their ink, I managed a smile as warmth flooded my heart.

The shop was doing quite well, far better than I'd expected, considering the amount of tat shops in Portland alone. We had a steady stream of clients Goose and

Knuckles had accumulated over the years, but we also had a nice uptick in new customers.

And Coop? Well, what red-blooded male didn't want a tat from my flawless demon?

She brought people to the shop in droves. They might show up wanting a tat from a hot babe, which, if you listened to the whispers and elbow jabs to each other's guts when a group of men came in, that was the general consensus for choosing Coop in the first place. But they left with some amazing artwork...and protection from demons courtesy of her special ink.

Yet another otherworldly topic we still hadn't openly discussed. I often pictured Coop in the bathroom sink back at our little guesthouse behind Knuckles's home, stirring up a witch's brew of some sorcery-filled recipe, but I hadn't actually asked where or how she came about the ink. I was simply grateful it existed—no questions asked.

With a sigh, my attention returned to the pictures on Coop's phone. Unfortunately, they revealed very little. Unless you count the fact that they rebranded the image in my mind of Sister Ophelia's dead body sprawled on the floor, while Deacon Delacorte held her and sobbed.

Sighing, I tucked Coop's phone away on the counter and decided texting Tansy was the next plan of action. Surely the coroner must have some preliminary thoughts on what had been used to strangle Sister Ophelia.

As I busied myself composing a text, the jingle of the bell over our etched-glass door made me look up. Higgs entered, with Jeff bounding alongside of him, his tongue hanging out the side of his mouth.

Higgs looked as tired as I felt. His tan face and gorgeous

dark eyes had lines embedded around them, and his usually sharp gaze looked bleary. His normally powerful strides toward me were labored and slightly sluggish, but he still smiled in my direction.

He patted the counter as Jeff ran circles around my legs. "Morning, Trixie. How are you today? Get any sleep?"

I fought a yawn. It was going to be a long day. "Not a wink. You?" I asked as I reached down and scratched Jeff's wiry fur.

Jeff was really doing a fairly decent job of playing the part of dog. Coop and I did our best to give him as much verbal interaction as we could when he was alone with us, and he was learning to keep his ability to speak to himself.

"Nope. I spent most of the night settling the men at the shelter. After their last scare with Dr. Fabrizio and that ape Griswald, they're worried a murderer is running loose again." He paused, an eyebrow raised. "Speaking of, have you heard from Tansy today?"

"I just sent her a text. How about you?"

"Nope. But I'd sure like to know what was used to strangle Sister Ophelia."

"So you think she was murdered, too?"

We hadn't talked much last night after they'd cleared the crime scene. We were both too depleted, I suspect. It really did take more out of you when you knew a murder victim personally.

Higgs had made sure I'd gotten home safely. And then he'd obviously spent the night at the shelter with the men who'd heard the trickle-down version of events, to try and keep them calm.

Higgs ran a hand over his freshly shaven face. "Is there any other possible scenario for the marks on her neck?"

"Exactly what I thought. So where do I start?"

"Where do *we* start?" he asked with a tired smile, the corners of his lips rising.

I planted my hands on my hips. "You're not going to give me a hard time about murderers and my possible decapitation while I stick my nose where it doesn't belong?"

He affected a look of astonishment, making his eyes go wide with a gasp. "I never used the word decapitation, Pretend Detective Lavender. I believe the word was *bludgeoned.* Which I'm pretty sure, at least once during your last *three* run-ins with a murderer, bludgeoning you to death was one of the methods of choice for ways to kill a nosy ex-nun."

I whipped a finger in the air to correct him. "Not true. One was drugs, the other was a gun, and the first one escapes me because it feels like it happened a hundred years ago."

Gosh, it really felt so long ago, I couldn't even remember the first murder I'd witnessed. Did that make me jaded?

Higgs sighed, long and dramatic, his chest inflating and pushing against the crisp white T-shirt he wore under a long-sleeved flannel. "I'm never, not for as long as I live, *ever* going to forget finding you broken and battered after almost having your organs removed by some madman. Don't mince words with me, young lady. I know what I said."

I shot him a teasing smile and leaned forward on the counter to grab my sketch pad. "Was he going to remove my organs? I suppose we'll never know."

Higgs leaned over the counter until he was at my eye level and stared at me dead on. "And I never *want* to know. I just want you safe. Either way, I'm here to help. I liked Sister Ophelia, too. She was nothing like the nuns I grew up with in Catholic school."

Ah. Another tidbit of information about Higgs I didn't know. I booped him on the nose with the tip of my finger and grinned.

"*You* went to Catholic school?"

"Yep. Ridiculous uniform and everything," he said, leaning back and letting his palms rest on the countertop with a grin. "Now, where to start? Thoughts on a way we can do this without stepping on Tansy's and Oz's toes?"

I held up the phone and showed him the text from Tansy. "Sister Ophelia taught English to the middle-school students in the seventh and eighth grades. I say we start there because Tansy's already been, which means we're free to go snooping unhindered by her requirements. Maybe we'll get lucky and find something she missed. It's an easy walk and it's a nice day. We might as well enjoy the kinder weather."

Higgs swept his hand toward the door. "Then let's do this."

I shot him a skeptical look. "Are you sure you're *my* Cross Higglesworth? I feel like we've been invaded by pod people and you're like copycat Higgs because the real Higgs was always giving me grief about my amateur investigations. He was never this affable about me poking around."

"Ah, yes. That. That was the old Higgs. The new Higgs has turned over a new leaf. And this new leaf says let's go steal some lunches and flash bright lights in those kids' eyes interrogation style for old time's sake."

I burst out laughing as I grabbed my purse from the shelf under the counter and threw the strap over my head. "That's horrible. This isn't like your days on the police force. They're only in middle school, Higgs. I doubt we'll have to interrogate them."

He pulled open the door of the shop. "Kids are hardcore these days and much more grown up than we ever were. They have way more tools than we did, too—like social media. Also, I bet you won't think I'm so horrible when I collect a stash of Ho Hos."

"Hah!" I barked. "Shows what you know. Kids don't eat Ho Hos anymore. All good moms would rather be drawn and quartered than give their children all those chemicals and preservatives. Kids these days come to school with bento boxes full of sushi rolls and dried kale."

He shook his head in mock disgust and rolled his eyes as I ducked under his arm and stepped out onto the cracked sidewalk. "Then is it any wonder they're all so intense? No growing teenager can live on kale alone, for Pete's sake. What happened to the good old days when we rode our bikes until it got dark and played in the woods?"

"Candy Crush was invented?"

He snorted a laugh before he instructed Jeff to stay with Coop and the guys. "Be a good boy, buddy. I'll be back soon."

As we made our way down the sidewalk, laughing about the differences in our childhoods compared to the children of today, I couldn't help but feel such relief that Higgs was all in on this investigation.

It didn't take us long before we strolled up to the school, an imposing brick structure with arched windows and beautiful stained-glass panels on either side of the doors, featuring various depictions of nature. There was also an enormous stone cross in the middle of the structure, at the peak of the building.

The day wasn't quite as warm as yesterday, but still pleasant enough, with a light breeze and people bustling up and down the adjacent sidewalk. Two large cherry blossom trees bracketed the front of the schoolyard, just waiting to bloom under the early spring sun.

Higgs stopped at the gates and wiped his brow. "Phew. I suddenly feel thirteen again."

I giggled as I pushed my way into the gates and headed toward the steps. "Does it feel like someone's about to steal your Ho Hos?"

"It feels like someone's about to come out of those doors and whack my knuckles with a ruler while she scolds me for writing on the bathroom wall."

I blinked with a gasp. "Did you write on the bathroom wall?"

He wagged a finger at me with a teasing smile. "Maybe. But I still don't think it warranted a whack over the knuckles with a ruler."

"Well, on behalf of my former sisters in the Lord, I apologize. I never would have whacked you or anyone with a ruler."

"Then nuns have gone soft in the new millennia, haven't they?"

I cupped my hand over my eyes, blocking out the bright

39

sun. "How many soft nuns do you know who don't shed a single tear when they get shot in the foot?"

"Touché," he said on a smile, and then he grabbed my arm. "Hey, any idea who we're even going to talk to? They don't just let anyone into a school anymore, let alone a private school. They have more rules than rules have rules. We need to know where we're going."

Shoot. I hadn't thought about that, but then I remembered something Sister Ophelia had told me. I pulled my phone out to check the time. "It's almost eleven o'clock. The eighth graders go for lunch at eleven. I know because Sister Ophelia sometimes dropped by Betty's to grab a cup of tea between classes. That's how we first met. We kept running into each other."

As if on cue, a bell rang and hordes of children began pouring out of the school, making me smile. I looked up to the sky and sent Sister Ophelia a silent thank you. She had to have been behind the timing on that one.

As the children flowed out, we pushed our way in, ducking between the eighth graders who were a whole lot bigger than they'd ever been in my day. The hall floors were shiny, lined with classroom doors in green and red, as more children in their blue school uniforms poured from them, chattering happily.

Which brought back mostly happy memories for me—happy until my days of debauchery, that is.

We stopped at a group of bright blue lockers while I tried to figure out where to go next.

My confusion must have showed. "Maybe we should find Sister Ophelia's classroom?" Higgs suggested. "There's bound to be someone taking over the class who can help us find out who the sister spent her time with. Maybe one of them knows something."

Out of nowhere, just ahead of us, a classroom door burst open, making a ruckus, leaving both Higgs and I leaning toward the sound.

A very large male, easily over six feet and riddled with muscle, launched himself down the hall. I only caught a glimpse of his face, hard and angry, before he put his head down and roared, "I didn't kill Sister Ophelia!"

As he barreled our way, his muscular legs encased in navy trousers, and armed with an uncanny sixth sense, because he swerved to avoid a nun who rather spryly ran behind him, he rammed right into Higgs. As a result, he knocked both of them to the ground with the force of his body.

But slamming into Higgs, who was equally as big, didn't even faze the man. Instead, he rose on all fours and did a quick crabwalk over him, his hands and feet slipping on the floor as he tried to get his footing.

And out of nowhere (honest to Pete, I don't know why I did what I did), I felt a surge of adrenaline. He might know something about Sister Ophelia's death, and that was all the fuel I needed to light a fire under my backside.

With a loud screech of an order to stop, I hurled myself at him as though springboards had sprouted in my sneak-ered feet. I felt the air hit my cheeks as I arced. I stretched my spine to reach as far as I could. I passed the row of lockers in a blur and smashed right onto his back, nailing him to the floor with my body.

And then I clung to his back, grabbing his wide shoulders and hanging on for dear life. "Don't move!" I hissed in his ear, pretty darn proud of myself.

Now listen, I don't want to brag, but I stuck that landing like I'd slathered myself in superglue. I'm not saying it didn't hurt to crash into a solid wall of flesh, because heaven and a surfboard, it surely did. My ribs were going to ache for days to come, right along with my face, because the latter did a rebound off his muscled back, making my head snap back.

But I did it, and now that I had him in my clutches, I wasn't letting go until he explained himself. Oh, and please note. I didn't even lose my purse in the melee. I have to tell you, I'm even prouder of that.

I'd knocked Gigantor to the ground and managed to keep my purse in the process.

Who's a soft nun now?

CHAPTER 4

The man struggled with me, trying to push me off, but I clung to him as though he were the last life raft on a sinking luxury liner. I wrapped my arm around his neck and pulled him toward me while he bucked, trying to shake me off.

"Trixie!" Higgs yelled, as I heard his feet scramble and thump against the floor.

More feet followed, and the swish of the nun's skirt when she raced toward me shortly thereafter, and I heard someone call out, "Daniel!"

Someone pulled me upward as Higgs grabbed hold of the perpetrator and asked gruffly, "Where do you want him, Sister?" he asked another nun who'd appeared on the scene.

I was still a little jarred after cracking my face against the man's back, but I managed to wobble my way toward a classroom, where Higgs sat him down in a chair he didn't quite fit in—and that was when I realized, this was no man, but a child.

His body might be the size of a freight train, but his face still had a bit of baby fat around his cheeks and neck.

Oh dear. I'd accosted a child.

Though, to be fair, I didn't know he was a child when he made a run for it, but I'd take my licks if someone called me on it.

The sister, a youngish woman, flushed and clearly panicked, flew toward him, her, red-hued hands outstretched. "Daniel! Are you all right? Are you hurt?"

"He's a student?" Higgs asked in astonishment.

"Yes," the weary-looking nun moaned. "This is Daniel Coletti."

I inhaled sharply. Now I had to add accosting a minor to my rap sheet. "Oh, I'm so sorry, Daniel. I didn't realize you were a student…"

But he clearly didn't want to hear my apologies. Daniel glared at us from his chair, his mouth thinning, his glittering blue eyes narrowed, and ran a hand through his bleached-blond hair. "I told you, I didn't kill Sister Ophelia, and I'm not saying anything else! I'm not gonna let you blame me for it!"

"No one is blaming you, Daniel!" the sister cried, wringing her hands. "We're simply asking you questions. Please calm down."

He folded his arms over his large chest and lifted his chin, his mood suddenly shifting from out-of-control to simmering rage. "I don't have to answer your questions if I don't want to!"

I looked at him—this enormous child in the body of a fully grown man, who, if he hadn't been left back, was no more than thirteen—amongst all the small desks and chairs with a backdrop of colorful posters hanging on the wall, and wondered why he was so angry.

He appeared almost resentful, and I had a sneaking suspicion he was often the fall guy for things he played no part in due to his size. Honestly, I didn't know they made them this big at thirteen, but coupled with what I guessed were parents who granted him plenty of leeway, he was the right mix of ingredients for one angry kid.

Another nun approached, looking as meek as the first, her hazel eyes imploring. "Daniel, we just want to understand why you were heard saying such awful things. We only want to help you."

Tapping his foot, he pushed back on the chair, leaning until it hit the side of a desk. "I said, I don't have to answer you! Why—won't—you—leave—me—alone?!" he bellowed, making my ears ring.

I caught a glimpse of Higgs, his jaw tightening, a sure sign he was having trouble not laying into this boy and giving him a real ex-cop's scare.

But I truly believed he behaved this way because he was frightened, rather than because he'd done anything so horrible.

"Daniel!" the sister with the pale hands reprimanded, though she was clearly afraid, making me wonder if she wasn't putting on a stern front for our benefit when, on the inside, she was a total marshmallow.

Daniel straightened as if he was going to flee, but Higgs gave him the "cop" look and said, "Don't even think about it, or I'll be the next one to tackle you. You'll stay put until I say otherwise."

Clearly, some order was necessary. Rather than

harangue Daniel, which, by the way he'd bolted, was what had happened before he'd burst out of the classroom, I decided introductions were in order.

I held out my hand to the sisters. "First, sisters? I'm Trixie Lavender—one-time nun from Saint Aloysius By The Sea. These days I own the tattoo shop over on Peach Street called Inkerbelle's. It's a pleasure to meet you both."

They each eyed me with clear hesitation, but took my hand in good faith. "Why are you here? Did you know Sister Ophelia?" the younger nun asked, her watery hazel eyes peering at me from beneath her wimple.

I nodded, tucking my purse behind me. "I did, and I was incredibly fond of her. We did some charity work together for Our Lady and Father Rico. On behalf of everyone at Inkerbelle's, I'm so sorry for your loss."

The other nun, a round, cheerful-looking lady with peachy skin and chubby hands, sniffled. "We all truly loved Sister Ophelia. I'm Sister Ann, by the way, and this is Sister Sue. Thank you for your kind words. We've all been in such a tizzy since we heard."

"I'm here to help with anything you need."

"Help?" Sister Ann asked, her full cheeks swallowed up in her tentative smile as she cocked her head.

"Oh, forgive me! In the chaos, I forgot to mention I'm here in sort of an unofficial capacity. I often help the Cobbler Cove Police with grief in the aftermath of a crime. You can call Detective Tansy Primrose to check, if you'd like."

Sister Sue nodded in affirmation, folding her hands in front of her. "Oh! She was just here asking questions, and she said you might drop by. Either way, I'm happy to help with whatever I can, no matter who asks."

"Then do you mind if I ask you some questions?" I asked, keeping my face passive and my tone light while totally ignoring the simmering Daniel, who sat but two desks away, fidgeting in his seat.

"Not at all," Sister Ann said in a hushed tone. "We're all so beside ourselves with shock, I think we haven't quite processed all our thoughts."

"Have Daniel's parents been called? Detective Primrose didn't mention Daniel's name when she listed the people she'd talked with, but they should be here."

Higgs shot me a strange look because he knew darn well Tansy hadn't sent me a list of anything. But listen, sometimes I get caught up in the moment. So I'm going to chalk it up to creative license if it gets me what I want. Sometimes, you have to improvise.

In my favor, she did say I could shadow her. Consider me shadowing.

Sister Ann nodded and cleared her throat. "We didn't know what Daniel had said until *after* Detective Primrose left, but they've been called, and I they should be arriving shortly." Then she shot a worried look to Sister Sue, leading me to believe Daniel's parents weren't the most involved.

I'd already knocked down a minor; it was probably best not to question him without a parent. Also, kids being kids, I knew my questions would pique his interest. So I waved them over to the part of the room by the sunny windows and grabbed three chairs while Higgs watched over Daniel.

As we sat, I noticed for the first time this was Sister Ophelia's classroom. There were pictures of her with the students at some kind of winter fair, and the books lined up on a shelf under the windows had her name on them.

Looking at both the women, their faces so full of sorrow, I sympathized. "First, again, let me tell you how sorry I am for your loss. Sister Ophelia was a wonderful, giving human being, and I'll miss her greatly."

"Us too," Sister Ann said. "I still can't believe this has happened. Who would want to hurt her?"

"Well, if you listen to the gossip, Daniel did!" Sister Sue replied with an almost angry tone, but then she looked around the room in guilt and thinned her lips.

I cocked my head. "Meaning?"

Sister Sue leaned toward me, her wimple brushing her shoulders. "Meaning one of the children, who I promised would remain anonymous, heard him threaten Sister Ophelia when she gave him an F on a report. He said, and I quote, 'I hate you so much I could kill you.'"

I blanched, as did the sisters, but it wasn't uncommon for kids his age to become dramatic and overreact to a situation. So I gave him a little leeway.

"So he was angry with Sister Ophelia for giving him a bad grade. Did this anonymous person say when this happened?"

Sister Sue inhaled and let out a shaky breath. "A few days before she was killed."

"Which would put this incident at last week," I muttered. "Did Sister Ophelia mention it to either of you? Or anyone, for that matter?"

Both sisters shook their heads.

"When did this anonymous source, who I'm assuming is a student, tell you about this incident?"

Sister Sue nodded vigorously. "Just after the police left today. She was frightened when she saw Detective Primrose and Officer Meadows. She said she was afraid if she didn't tell us, Daniel would get away with a sin and go to Hell."

Now I nodded. Boy, did I know what the threat of fire and damnation could do to your head. "Would you consider talking to this anonymous source again? Or possibly letting us talk to whoever this is? I promise we'll keep this in the strictest of confidences."

Sister Ann's eyes went wide. "I'll do it," she volunteered, but she didn't offer anything else, and I didn't press. I didn't want to pressure her to break a confidence on our account. Not yet anyway.

"So, is Daniel hard to manage? Is he a hothead, or is this an isolated incident?"

"Daniel's always been…difficult. Yes. That's probably the best word to describe him. He's not a bad child, just mismanaged and left to his own devices more often than not," Sister Sue chimed in. "Sister Ophelia loved him. She loved all her students, Trixie, no matter how difficult. She probably didn't tell anyone about the threat because she knew he didn't truly mean it."

I sighed and clapped my hands against my thighs before I rose. "Well, thank you for telling me. I won't take up any more of your time, but I suggest you call Detective Primrose and tell her exactly what you shared with me. She'll need to know."

As I began to wend my way through the chairs toward the door, two expensively dressed people flew in and ran to Daniel. The clack of high heels and the cloud of very blonde hair, coupled with an air of arrogance, told me who they were before they spoke a word.

The Colettis, I presumed.

Daniel's mother, draped in a fur coat and smelling of pricey perfume, dropped down next to him and cupped his chin, never taking off her sunglasses. "Are you all right, sweetie?"

But he jerked his face away in distaste and sighed with exasperation—typical for most children that age, I suppose. "I'm fine. Get off me, Mom."

His father, a short but incredibly imposing man in a classically cut, black pinstriped business suit, slapped his son on the back. "Don't talk to your mother like that, Daniel," he ordered sharply, making me instantly feel sorry for the boy when his face fell and his shoulders slumped.

I decided to save him some humiliation and approach his parents. "Mr. and Mrs. Coletti?"

Mrs. Coletti lifted her chiseled chin and pushed her short blonde bob from her face. "*Who* are you?" she asked, looking down her nose at me from behind her dark sunglasses.

I suppose, me in my drab jeans and pilling gray sweater, I came off as beneath her, judging from the way she was dressed, but I straightened my spine and squared my shoulders.

Holding out my hand, I smiled. "I'm Trixie Lavender. I own the tattoo shop over on Peach Street." I don't know why I said that. People of this ilk didn't frequent places like mine, but it felt important to let them know. "I am...*was* a good friend of Sister Ophelia's. Do you mind if I ask Daniel some questions?"

Mr. Coletti pushed his wife behind him with a nudge and gave me a blistering glance, his sharp blue eyes never leaving my face. "Never mind what she wants. *I* mind if you ask Daniel some questions. What is this about?"

"This is about a threat your son made toward Sister Ophelia," Higgs countered, using his cop voice. I knew it well. It was authoritative and brisk and meant he wasn't going to be unsettled by Mr. Sharp-Dressed-Man.

Mr. Coletti had to look upward at Higgs, but he gave him a scathing once over to silently assure Higgs that he was neither intimidated nor afraid of his size. "And you are?"

Higgs stuck out a hand and caught them all off guard by grinning. "Cross Higglesworth."

Mrs. Coletti virtually melted into the floor, her breathing fluttering in and out of her lungs. She placed her hand in Higgs's and lingered for a good long moment before he pulled his hand from her grip.

But Mr. Coletti wasn't as charmed as his wife. He didn't take Higgs's hand. In fact, he ignored it, grabbing Daniel by the arm and trying to yank him upward.

"I don't care who you two are. No one's asking my son anything without an attorney present. Now, get up, Daniel. We're going home!"

Daniel pulled his arm from his father's grip, but he rose and gave us all a dirty look before sauntering toward the door. I think if he could have gotten away with sticking his tongue out at us, he would have.

"Now, if you want to ask my son questions, you'll do it with an attorney present and not before!" he barked, and I almost expected him to click his heels together like the guy on *Hogan's Heroes* before he grabbed Mrs. Coletti by the arm and ushered her out.

As they left the room, the air felt as though it returned and we all stared at each other for a moment, collecting our thoughts.

I finally asked, "Is Mr. Coletti always so curt?"

Sister Ann let out a cleansing breath and nodded. "He's always very angry about something. I don't think I've ever seen him smile. Not once."

"I almost can't blame the kid for being so edgy with a father like that," Higgs commented under his breath.

Nodding, I decided we were done here. There was nothing left to ask if we couldn't talk to Daniel or this anonymous source.

"They do say you are your environment, and he's certainly a product of a rigid upbringing, if Mr. Coletti's any indication. By the way, sisters, what does Mr. Coletti do for a living?"

Sister Sue twisted her fingers together. "He's a very expensive, very well-known divorce attorney...and gracious, he makes me a nervous wreck."

Well, that explained his super-expensive suit and hawk-like gaze. "And Mrs. Coletti? What does she do?"

Both the nuns looked at one another, mischief in their eyes. "Shop," they said in unison.

I tipped my head back and laughed, handing them a card from Inkerbelle's so they could give me a call if they remembered anything else, and then we said our goodbyes.

We strolled down the quiet hall together, both of us lost in our thoughts. I was processing what Daniel has said to

Sister Ophelia, when I heard Sister Ann call out to us to wait.

Turning, we both looked at each other as she approached, her footsteps padding softly against the floor. But she looked panicked as she reached out and grabbed my hand.

Breathless, she said, "I didn't want to say anything in front of Sister Sue, but two things before you go, if you don't mind?"

I felt her anxiety, and it left me feeling anxious, too. "Of course, Sister Ann."

She swallowed hard then looked me in the eye. "First, Daniel isn't just difficult. He's a bully, and I suppose I understand why he behaves the way he does. His father isn't a pleasant man. He's always goading Daniel and pushing him. I don't think I've ever heard him speak a kind word to the child. But Daniel's infamous for stealing lunches and constantly picking fights. Naturally, he's the size of a grown man, so he frightens the other children. Sister Ophelia always took his side when we suggested suspension. She thought he was just misunderstood."

That sounded like Sister Ophelia. Always rooting for the underdog even while seeing them for what they were.

"Okay, and is there more? You said there were two things."

Sister Ann blew out a breath, her cheerfully round face clearly displaying how torn she was to impart her next bit of information. "I overheard Sister Ophelia arguing with someone."

My ears instantly perked up, but it was Higgs who asked, "With who?"

"I don't know who it was, and I never, ever would have said a word if Sister Ophelia didn't end up...well, you know how she ended up..." She shook her head and looked at me, her eyes pleading and brimming with tears she impatiently brushed away. "Anyway, I don't know who it was. I didn't recognize the other voice. I couldn't hear the conversation clearly, except for the words 'no one can ever know.' I know it was a female, and I'm almost positive it was another nun because Sister Ophelia said, 'I saw you with my own eyes. You've broken your commitment to God. When you became a nun, you made a promise to be faithful to *Him*.'"

CHAPTER 5

*M*y mouth fell open, but no words would come out and my poker face went on the lam. Sure, I'd heard of things like this happening, but I'd never visited the scenario up close and personal.

Thankfully, Higgs had my back and stepped in. "So she was having a conversation with someone who'd broken their vows? Using the words 'faithful to *Him*' implies someone was behaving indiscreetly. As in an affair?"

Sister Ann's hands flapped upward in a nervous flutter of fingers as her eyes darted around the hallway. "I think so, and that's all I know. I mean, it could have a million different meanings, right? The bit about faithfulness and commitment? It doesn't have to mean an affair, does it? But I left as fast as I could because you know what the Good Book says about gossip, Trixie. Besides, I didn't want to hear any more. I despise knowing things I shouldn't. But when I heard what happened to Sister Ophelia, I knew I had to tell someone if the information helps with the investigation."

When I finally found my voice, I gripped the strap of my purse and asked, "Where did this argument happen, Sister Ann? Here at school?"

She bounced her head and toyed with her rosary. "In the coat closet by the entryway. The door was closed, but they were yelling, which is why I heard them in the first place. Most everyone had gone for the day, but I stayed later to do some lesson planning for the following week." She looked over her shoulder in her nervousness and whispered, "Oh! I can't tell you how much I regret hearing that conversation!"

I patted her arm to reassure her she was right to have told me. "But you're doing the right thing, Sister Ann. I know it doesn't feel like it, but the person responsible for this can't be caught if we don't have all the facts. So tell me, what day did this happen?"

"Friday after school let out."

And that was definitely within the time frame for Sister Ophelia's murder, which occurred over the weekend.

"Thank you, Sister Ann. If you think of anything else, anything at all, please call me. And do call Detective Primrose and share what you know. This is important information." I gave her hand one last squeeze and turned to leave, my head whirring.

As we exited the school, the children were setting up a memorial for Sister Ophelia by the fence, with her picture and candles. My heart promptly constricted in my chest and more tears threatened to fall.

Higgs pulled my hand into his and guided me past them. "So that just got sticky, huh? Do you think Sister Ophelia meant this nun was having an affair?"

"I don't know. It's not like it doesn't happen, because I

assure you, it does. Priests and nuns break their vows sometimes. They're human, too."

"Okay, so we need to find out who Sister Ophelia was
arguing with."

But I frowned. "And what about Daniel? Do you really
think he's capable of strangling someone? That's a vengeful
act, Higgs. He's just a kid."

"Well, he's certainly big enough, Trixie. He's strong as an
ox," Higgs reminded me as we walked to the corner.

"Tell me about it. But seriously, would he be out that late
on a Sunday night? Deacon Delacorte found Sister Ophelia
at about ten o'clock. He's only thirteen, for pity's sake."

Higgs shrugged his wide shoulders. "Do you suppose
anyone's watching him that closely to know what he's
doing?"

"Listen, the Colettis might not win parents of the year,
but surely they'd know if their son was out that late on the
night before a school day."

He stopped at the crosswalk and pressed the button, his
eyebrows knitting together in a frown. "Would they know if
they were passed out drunk?"

"*What?*"

"Mrs. Coletti. She reeked of booze, Trixie. No one
drinks this early in the day on a Monday unless they drink
all the time, at all hours of the day."

"You could smell her breath?"

Gosh. I had so much more to learn—so much more to
observe than just the obvious. I could kick myself for
forgetting to use all my senses.

He wiggled an eyebrow and winked. "Well, she did pull
me in so close I could see her tonsils."

I barked a laugh. "She sure did. Boy, the ladies are just lining up for you these days, huh? Carla, and now Mrs. Coletti."

"Ah. But they're not the *right* ladies," he said with his devastatingly handsome smile. "Anyway, Mrs. Coletti drinks. So maybe she wasn't aware Daniel even left the house, and I'd bet Mr. Coletti works all kinds of odd hours, being a high-powered divorce attorney. Plus, it's not improbable for a kid his age to sneak out. From the size of him, I can't believe he hasn't rented his own apartment by now."

I chuckled. "He *is* a big kid. I swear, Higgs, I had no idea he was a child when I lunged for him. At a quick glance, he looked like an adult."

Higgs held out his fist for me to bump. "Impressive tackle, by the way."

I bumped his fist with mine, but I shook my head as we crossed the street. "I'm not a fan of this theory, Higgs. Not even a little. Daniel behaves the way he does because he got a crummy lot in life with his parents, but I don't believe he'd kill Sister Ophelia for a bad grade, even if he said he wanted to."

"But what about if your parents pressured you all the time? What if your father was a rich, prominent attorney who would give you the business if your grades weren't good? I get the feeling Mr. Coletti, whose first name is Horatio by the way, I Googled him, would use extreme measures to keep his son in line. Measures that might frighten Daniel enough to resort to extreme measures himself."

I firmly shook my head. "Still not buyin' what you're sellin'."

"You're doing the soft thing again."

"You mean assuming the victim's emotions?" We'd talked about avoiding this since I began to work with Tansy, and I constantly warred with my head and my heart.

He nodded. "Yep. Sister Ophelia was fond of Daniel. You don't want her to be wrong about him because you liked her and you trusted her judgment. So you're making up excuses for Daniel instead of looking at the entire picture with objectivity."

That was certainly a fair observation, and one I'd try to keep in perspective. "Okay, but we have no proof of anything until we actually talk to him anyway. I don't know if that's ever going to happen after our experience this morning. So let's move on to whomever Sister Ophelia was talking to in the closet. I guess we can safely say this alleged nun was having an affair."

"And how did Sister Ophelia find out about it? Did this nun just spill the beans or did Sister Ophelia catch her in the act?"

I think I went a whiter shade of pale. As I said, things of that sordid nature do happen in the church, probably more than any of us were ever aware, but I can't imagine catching someone in the act and having to live with either keeping it a secret or telling someone.

"She did say she *saw her*. Maybe she witnessed whoever this nun was, catting around and she confronted her? Maybe that's why Sister Ophelia was so stressed? Stressed enough to smoke a cigarette not once, but twice in one day. When I went to take the trash out to the dumpster while we were setting up for the speed dating, she was smoking, and she told me she only did it when she was stressed. Foolish me, I didn't ask her what she was stressed about because we got distracted by Carla Ratagucci's fundraising tactics."

Higgs drove his hands into his pockets. "Maybe she wanted to talk to Father Rico about it? Remember, he did say she wanted to talk to him just before the event, something Sister Patricia confirmed, but he'd been too busy with preparing announcements."

"So you're saying she was going to tattle?" My glance at him was skeptical. "I gotta tell you, Higgs, that doesn't sound like Sister O. She was a problem solver, and she had a kind heart. If there was some kind of physical affair going on, it definitely meant trouble for the parties involved, but I don't believe Sister Ophelia would say anything and break a confidence before she at least tried to help the person. If she was going to tell Father Rico, the situation was more dire than the bits and pieces Sister Ann heard."

"But it's definitely a moral dilemma, especially for a nun, yes? Maybe she was going to keep it vague when she talked to Father Rico? Hypothetical circumstances and such?"

"Maybe. Either way, we can't eliminate that lead."

"Or the lead to Daniel," he reminded me once more, and I'm certain it was in an effort to keep me grounded.

As we wandered down the sidewalk in the faint sun, passing people and the places I'd come to love, looking into every face with suspicion, I wondered for the millionth time, who would kill a nun loved by so many, so brutally?

And why?

*W*e'd gathered at Knuckles's for our biweekly meal—the one where we all brought something and shared our goodies in potluck fashion.

As we sat around the table, I waited to hear something from Tansy after sending her what I'd learned, if she didn't already know, that is. But so far there'd been nothing. Nothing about Daniel, nothing about any unusual evidence from the crime scene not visible to the naked eye—nothing about what was used to kill Sister Ophelia—just a big fat nothing.

Coop sat next to me, eating her stroganoff with relish, but we weren't our usual noisy bunch tonight. Normally, we spent our meals chatting about current events or telling stories about our days. But tonight, our somber mood lingered over us like a dark cloud.

Goose, sitting on the other side of me, tapped my hand with a gnarled finger. "Have we thought about a memorial for Sister Ophelia, Trixie?"

I wiped my mouth and sighed. As good as Goose's creamy beef stroganoff was, I just wasn't hungry. "I didn't want to interfere with any plans Father Rico might have, but some of the parishioners are meeting tonight at eight for a candlelight memorial. I thought I might go, if you'd like to join me."

Goose bobbed his do-rag-covered head and wiped his mouth with his napkin. "You bet I do. I'm sure we all do. But we'd better get cleaned up if we're gonna make it."

Nodding, I pushed my chair back and began to gather dishes. My heart was so heavy tonight. I'm sure my sudden low had a lot to do with how tired I was, but I found myself fighting the urge to break out in a fit of tears.

"Trixie?" Coop said, bringing in a stack of dishes and placing them on the counter. "Did you learn anything at the school today?"

We hadn't had a chance to talk since my return after speaking with the sisters. Coop had been busy with tattoo appointments all afternoon, and I'd been busy sketching for some upcoming clients.

I shrugged my shoulders as I began rinsing dishes and Higgs rolled up his sleeves to stack them in the dishwasher. "We found out some interesting stuff, for sure. I don't know that it has anything to do with Sister Ophelia's murder, though."

"What she means, Coop, is she doesn't *want* what we found to have anything to do with Sister Ophelia's murder," Higgs corrected with a teasing smile.

I made a face at him and explained to Coop what we'd learned.

Coop began wiping down Knuckles's glossy counters, but she nodded her head when I was through.

"I know you won't like this, Trixie, but I think Higgs is correct. You're allowing your feelings to cloud your judgment. This Daniel sounds like a prime suspect. I wouldn't take him off the list until you have absolute proof he's innocent."

Sighing, I almost agreed. Each time I relayed what Daniel said, it sounded worse to my ears.

"I'm not discounting him entirely, I'm just relegating him to the back burner for now."

Yes, that sounded like a big fat excuse, but my gut was talking, and I was trying to listen.

Knuckles gave my shoulders a squeeze, pulling me against his burly side and dropping a kiss on the top of my head.

"Trixie girl, you're a good egg, but I'm gonna agree with everyone else here. This kid sounds like he's capable of killing someone."

"Okay, okay," I conceded, patting him on his round belly, but I still didn't like it because it didn't feel right, my feelings of sympathy for Sister Ophelia aside. "How about we focus on getting to the candlelight vigil for Sister Ophelia and talk about the rest of this later?"

"Deal," Knuckles agreed. "And guys? Don't worry about the rest of this, I'll clean it up when we get back."

But Coop shook her head as she pulled her auburn hair up on top of her head and secured it with a rubber band. "No, Knuckles. That's not how we do it. We clean up after ourselves, especially when we're in someone else's home. It means we respect them, and I definitely respect you."

Knuckles tweaked her cheek and grinned, dropping a kiss on the top of her head, too. "I like you, too, Coopie."

She stared up at him, and I knew she was trying to smile on the outside, the way her heart was smiling on the inside.

I loved that Coop was so free with her heart. She never held back a compliment or any of the emotions she was beginning to experience. In most cases, that was a good thing. Though, I wondered if there wouldn't come a time when she would need to keep her cards closer to her chest.

For now, I'd just admire her freedom to express herself and revel in the fact that, each day, she made a new milestone and became more and more a part of this family of strays we'd patched together.

On that note, I needed some air before this candlelight vigil. Calling Jeff, I grabbed his leash and latched it to his collar. "I'll take Jeff for a walk before we go."

"Thanks, Trixie," Higgs called over his broad shoulder from the kitchen as I opened the door and ran down the steps, with Jeff pulling me the entire way.

Jeff loved to walk, and I was happy to accommodate. Not only was it good for me to get my heart pumping, but it allowed Jeff to be the real him. He could talk to Coop and me, express any worries or troubles he was having with us as his sounding board, before he had to go back to his life as someone's pet.

I blew out a breath as we strolled along our darkened neighborhood, tired and worried that I hadn't heard anything from Tansy about Daniel or Sister Ann.

"You okay there, Trix?" Jeff asked in his light Bostonian accent as he lifted his leg on his favorite maple tree. Who am I kidding, all the trees lining the street were Jeff's favorite.

"I'm fine, Jeff," I whispered, sitting on my haunches to give him a hug around his neck. "How are you these days? I feel like I haven't checked in enough."

He nuzzled my cheek and licked my nose. "As good as can be expected when you're stuck in a dog's body. But the real question is, how are you? I'm wicked sorry about the sister. She used to sneak me scraps of her lunch all the time when she came to help feed the guys at the shelter."

I scratched his ears and smiled at his concern for me. Jeff was stuck in the body of a dog with the sometime mentality of a twelve-year-old, but he was as sweet as pie, and if not for he and Livingston, I'm not sure anyone would have found us the night both Coop and I were kidnapped by Dr. Fabrizio and Detective Griswald. I'd never forget that as long as I lived.

"Determined to figure out who killed her, is how I am. Which, speaking of, can you keep an ear out tonight at the vigil? No one suspects the unassuming dog. You're kind of my ace in the hole," I teased.

He circled my legs, brushing up against me as he wound around my calves. "Aw, you don't think Sister Ophelia's killer will show up to the vigil, do ya?"

As the wind picked up, I shivered and tucked my sweater around me a little tighter, watching the shadows from the branches play against the houses along the street.

"I've heard some killers go back to the scene of the crime. So anything's possible, Jeff, but what I really want to know is if anyone knows about this nun who was having an affair. I think that's more likely to come up in conversation than the killer showing."

"An affair, huh? You can bet for sure I'll keep an ear out and report back to ya if I hear anything worth repeating. But maybe I won't have to. Maybe you'll sketch something like you did the last time you were huntin' a killer. That was ca-ra-zy pants."

Closing my eyes, I could only hope that were true. The last murder, the demon in me (we'd finally discovered his name is Artur), rather than become violent and unruly, had instead, through me, sketched what he'd seen the night Dr. Mickey, a local dentist, was killed. It had turned out to be very helpful once we understood what the heck it all meant.

But I hadn't had an attack in months now, and my sketches were done without the aid of Artur. Don't get me wrong, I know he's still lurking in there, his greasy black claws firmly latched on to my soul, but life had been quite peaceful since the mess with Dr. Fabrizio.

I can't say that makes me unhappy, even though I know I need to spend some serious time investigating what's going on inside me. I wanted to believe Artur would up and disappear so I didn't have to think about exorcisms and all manner of supernatural goings on. But I also knew that was as unlikely as me ever being allowed to return to the church as a nun.

"We'll see, but I wouldn't count on it. It's been a while since I last sketched with Artur as my guide. So for now, just be my eyes and ears, okay?"

"You bet, Trix. Promise me one thing though?"

"Anything. Well," I added on a chuckle, "*almost* anything. There'll be no more sausage for you on my watch, buddy. I want to indulge the human in you as much as the next person, but that was a complete mess and it stunk to high heaven."

Jeff let his head hang between his shoulders as he sniffed the sidewalk. "Ugh. That was wicked bad. Didn't feel right for days."

Chuckling once more, I nodded and wrinkled my nose. "It sure was. I didn't think we'd ever get the smell out of the throw rug in the living room. Anyway, what do you want me to promise, buddy?"

"Promise you'll stay safe. If this person's out there, whackin' *nuns*, he'll whack just about anyone in his path. I don't want that anyone to be you. I only have you guys, unless you wanna tell Higgs I can talk. I don't know what the heck I'd do if I couldn't talk to you and Coopie, and even that flappy-mouth feather coat on wheels of yours. I'd miss ya somethin' awful."

Dropping a kiss on his head before rising, I whispered, "I love you, Jeff."

"I love you, too, Trix."

As we walked back to Knuckles's, passing the houses of our neighbors in all their Craftsman glory, seeing the heads of tulips poking out from various lighted gardens, I sent up a silent request to Sister Ophelia.

Hey, up there, Sister Ophelia. I hope you're settling in and there's plenty of Unsolved Mysteries to watch. I know you'll rule the roost in no time flat. But while you get situated and establish supremacy over the remote control, some ideas on who killed you would be most appreciated.

Miss you,

Trixie

CHAPTER 6

*C*oop and I stood outside Our Lady of Perpetual Grace by the long string of steps leading to the doors, candles in hand as a light mist of rain began. Goose and Knuckles were off somewhere in the crowd, while Higgs stood with some of the men from the shelter who were still having trouble dealing with the death of their beloved Sister Ophelia and the fear of a killer on the loose.

So many people had shown up to pay their respects, from the children at Our Lady's middle school, accompanied by their parents, to parishioners galore.

Carla Ratagucci waved to me, her eyes shiny with tears. Even Carla, who'd sparred with my favorite nun, had loved her. My fervent hope, despite my misgivings about the existence and rules of Heaven, was that Sister Ophelia had grabbed a soft, cushy cloud to sit on while her legs dangled and she watched all these devoted people gathered in her honor.

As each battery-operated candle illuminated, the sidewalk dotted with light and the hushed voices of mourners, I swallowed back more tears. I wasn't looking forward to saying goodbye.

My tired mind continued to twirl theory after theory around in my fried brain, but I kept coming up with the one answer I didn't like. It was entirely possible Daniel had killed Sister Ophelia.

He had motive. He had the strength. He likely had the opportunity, if what Higgs said about his negligent parents was true.

"Miss Marple." Tansy drawled her nickname for me in my ear. "How are we this eve, love?"

I gave her a bleak smile but found myself warmed by her concern. "Tired. How goes the investigation?"

"Like molasses uphill in the winter. I'm still waiting on prelims from the coroner about what was used to strangle the old gal. It surely wasn't anything obvious. Nothing—not to my naked eye, anyway—was visible on her neck. Whatever it was, it didn't cut her skin. Yet whoever did it was strong—incredibly strong."

Those words made me think of Daniel, and I had to fight a cringe. "Did you talk to Daniel?"

"I bloody well did," she scoffed in disgust, scuffing her feet against the rippled sidewalk and squinting off into the distance. "What a three-ring circus that turned into. His parents, some lot of nonces they are, eh?"

Nodding, I shook my head in complete understanding. The more I heard about the Colettis, the more I sympathized with Daniel's plight. "Ah, so I guess you were treated to the Colettis' special brand of snobbery? Lovely pair, aren't they?"

She scoffed again and made a face, the glow of the candlelight illuminating her aggravation. "They're certainly no treat, love. They definitely thought us hoi polloi if I ever did see."

I gave her a confused glance. "*Hoi who?*"

"Hoi polloi, you Yank," she teased with a swift wink. "It means they thought we were nothing more than mere commoners."

I smiled and nodded. "Like I said. Snobs. Anyway, Daniel…?"

"Yes, the lad. He has a solid alibi for where he was the night Sister Ophelia was murdered."

I gripped the candle tight and held my breath. "Where was he?"

"In a private jet on his way back from some fundraiser his parents hosted in Vancouver, BC. La-di-da, eh?"

"And it's a solid alibi? No if, ands or buts?"

"Solid as Jason Momoa's abs, darling."

My shoulders sagged in relief and every muscle in my body enjoyed a brief respite. "I hate to tell you, but I'm glad to hear that. I know it doesn't bring us any closer to the killer, but I talked to the sisters at the school today, and they told me he has it pretty rough with those two for parents."

"Hah! I don't doubt that. Getting them to speak to me, even when it was in the lad's best interest, was like making an appointment with the good Lord himself. Mr. Coletti had a whole team of attorneys lined up before we could ask him a simple question. And the Missus? Oi! Smelled like my old vicar after a night of vespers."

So Tansy had noticed her drinking, too? I really was off my game. "Okay, so we can cross him off our list. Did you speak to Sister Ann? Did she tell you what she heard in the coat closet at the school? I told her to call you with the information."

"She did, and we're going to canvass all the nuns again tomorrow. Maybe someone else heard, too. Someone must know if one of the other nuns is a little loosey-goosey, shouldn't they? Gossip spreads like wildfire in the church, I hear. They're a bit like hospitals. Doctors and nurses are always having affairs."

I tried not to bristle at the suggestion my former kind were all like a batch of dirty birds, breaking their vows left and right, but the part about gossip couldn't be denied. There was plenty of that to go around, even if it was mostly harmless chatter.

In fact, I'd bet my bippy I'd been the subject of plenty of wagging tongues once I'd skulked off from St. Aloysius, so I couldn't deny gossip existed.

Tansy must have noticed me cringe, because she rubbed my arm and threw me an apologetic glance.

"Bah, that came out wrong, Trixie. My apologies."

"Not necessary. I understand we see the landscape of the church from very different perspectives. There is a lot of chatter from the peanut gallery, that's true and affairs do happen. But if what Sister Ann said is correct, that's a bigger scandal than *I've* ever seen up close and personal. At Saint Aloysius, the most scandalous thing to happen was when Sister Bettina used her rosary to fish a bobby pin from the toilet. We talked about that for days on end."

Tansy's chuckle was low as the wind whispered through her hair. "Though, definitely not the same as murder. Anyway, we're talking to everyone at this point and doing

71

all the appropriate background checks. We even did one on Father Rico."

The wind began to really pick up, making me regret not bringing a warmer jacket. I tucked my chin into the neck of my hoodie. "And?"

"Did you know he wasn't always a priest? He used to work at a gas station in Kansas City, Missouri, back in the late '80s."

"Really?" But then I shrugged. That wasn't as uncommon a story as one would think. "It doesn't surprise me, though. Lots of people come to faith later in life."

"Indeed. Though, can't say as I blame him for turning to the church after what he went through."

I didn't know a lot about Father Rico's background other than he'd been at Our Lady Since the early 2000s and he was a friend of Higgs's. "Went through? What happened to him?"

"He was held hostage by some disgruntled employee of the gas station he worked for. Mind you, negotiations went on with his captor for twenty-two bloody hours."

"That's awful! Poor Father Rico. I had no idea his past was so tragic. Did they catch the guy who held him hostage?"

She gave me one of her direct gazes. "He's dead. Taken out by a sharpshooter on the scene."

"Any lingering angry family members who hold Father Rico responsible for the death of a loved one?"

Goodness knew, I'd seen plenty of victim blaming in the first case I'd been caught up in with Higgs, and even some of the cases I went on with Tansy. It wasn't unheard of for a family member to hold the person their loved one harmed responsible for their death.

She winked at me and nudged my shoulder before she pulled her phone out of her blazer pocket. "You're thinking more like a copper every day, Trixie love." She showed me her phone, and an article she'd pulled up from the *Kansas City Star*. "Only one remaining survivor to the hostage-taker—whose name was Leslie Turner, as a by the by. The relative was his mother, and she died ten years ago of heart failure. His was the usual MO. Loner, angry, sullen. Read the article about it. That's how I know Father Rico went off to seminary after that. He said, and I quote, 'Angels surrounded me and held me in their arms the entire time I was held hostage. I was never afraid once because I knew the Lord would keep me safe.'"

"Wow," I whispered in awe as I skimmed the article. That was some real, true faith. The kind of faith I wasn't so sure I still had not just in my head, but deep in my heart. "He's a wonderful vessel for the Lord. I can tell you true, his sermons are full of love and hope, and I'm so glad he found his calling. But that still leaves us at square one. I mean, that's if you're certain Leslie Turner has no angry loved ones, looking to exact revenge by way of killing Father Rico's crew."

"Not a one, and Deacon Cameron and Deacon Dela-corte? Also clean as whistles, but it wouldn't hurt to have a chat with them if you're up to it. They were both a little on edge today, which is totally understandable, given their colleague was so brutally murdered."

My shoulders went back to sagging. "I don't get it, Tansy."

Tansy scratched her head and nodded. "Me either, love. I just can't figure who'd want to kill a harmless nun…and that makes me wonder if she didn't have secrets no one knew about."

"If she did, I didn't know them, if that's what you're asking. We were very friendly, but we didn't confide anything no one else knew." Well, almost anyway. Sighing about my own secrets, I asked, "What about the CCTV? Anything of interest?"

"There isn't one in the alleyway by the exit door, but we did check the surrounding areas, and so far, nothing suspicious. Not even remotely suspicious, matter of fact."

People had begun to assemble at the steps of the church by Sister Ophelia's smiling picture along, with Father Rico, who I assumed would say a few words. There'd be no burial until Sister Ophelia's body was released, but mourners sometimes needed a religious rite of passage—a symbolic event to ease their grief. This would have to do for now.

"Well, thanks, Tansy. I appreciate you keeping me up to date. I'll talk to the deacons and see what I can learn. Though, I will tell you, I don't know how much they'll open up. Deacon Cameron's a little awkward with me due to my ex-nun status, if you'll pardon the description. I think he thinks I decided to leave the church to follow Satan. He takes a wide berth with me. And Deacon Delacorte is new. He just arrived a few days ago. He might not feel comfortable talking to me."

Tansy rubbed my arm and smiled warmly, her specialty when she knew I was afraid I'd fail. "Everyone is comfortable talking to you, Miss Marple. That's just who you are, love. But you do as you see fit. Not a fig of pressure you'll get from me."

"Thanks, Tansy. You're the best boss who doesn't pay me *ever*."

Tansy chuckled as she started to take her leave. "There's my favorite sassy pants. Bravo, Miss Marple. Now, I'm off to canvass and keep a watchful eye for anyone suspicious because...?" she asked with a coaxing tone.

"Because sometimes the killer will return to the scene of the crime to watch it all play out," I replied dutifully.

She grinned and bobbed her blonde head. "Good on ya, Trixie Lavender. Now, if you need me, for anything at all, love, just text and I'm there."

"Thanks, Tansy," I whispered into the blowing wind as she wound her way through the crowd and disappeared.

Someone handed Father Rico a mic and as he began to speak, I found myself watching everyone's faces, most with tears pouring down their cheeks, and still I wondered who'd killed a nun, who everyone appeared to love, with such brutal force?

"Fair maiden," a voice whispered in my ear. "'Tis I. Here to pay my respects to the beloved Sister Ophelia of the fine establishment Our Lady of Perpetual Grace."

I knew Solomon was in my midst even before he spoke because of his scent. I think he'd missed his shower time this week. We'd talked about the importance of cleanliness on many occasions, but Solomon was the captain of his own ship.

As I peered into his face, lined with many a battle scar from living on the streets, I noted his eyes were soft with sympathy. He'd even removed his Viking hat and left his grocery cart full of his favorite things parked somewhere other than here at the vigil. So okay, he hadn't taken a shower, but he had attempted to show respect in his own way, and that made me proud.

Though, he was using his medieval speak as his safety net, which meant he was feeling insecure and scared.

So I played along the way I always do because I know it makes him comfortable. "Aye, my liege. I'm so happy to see you here. It shows how much you respected the lovely Sister Ophelia. She liked you a great deal, you know."

"Aye," he mumbled, letting his scruffy chin drop to his chest as he drove his usually fluttering hands into the pockets of his tattered peacoat. "Sister O was kind, she was. She... She told me I was beautiful, and God loves me just the way I am. She did. She said that."

Tears stung my eyes and the wind bit my skin. That sounded like Sister Ophelia. She'd been partial to Solomon due to his essentially undiagnosed autism. She worried for him, lit candles for him at mass to keep him safe from harm. She'd even bought him his favorite Gobstopper candies from time to time because she knew he loved them.

"Sister Ophelia was indeed a good soul, and she cared about your well-being, Solomon. I'm glad you came to pay your respects. I know she'd like that."

He looked at me then, imploring me with his glistening eyes. "Can I stand next to you, Trixie? Will you hold my hand?"

When Solomon felt his most unsafe, he reached out for human contact. It wasn't often, but I knew he needed to share his sadness so it wouldn't overwhelm him.

My heart constricted and tightened as I held out my

hand to him. "Of course, Solomon. You can always hold my hand."

His fingers fluttered against mine before he pressed them against the back of my hand, which I suppose was Solomon's idea of holding my hand. Whatever made him comfortable was fine with me.

As Father Rico continued his soothing words and talked about how valuable Sister Ophelia was to the congregation and the church, I absorbed them, allowed them into my heart, and tried to decipher this tragedy by using the balm the father poured out over us.

We all were deeply invested in Father Rico's words—he had an incredible way of expressing what we were all feeling. In fact, we were so invested, the scream we heard, the one that eventually made us all turn around, took a few seconds before it sank in.

But when it did, it stayed with me for days afterward.

The sound of Carla Ratagucci, screaming so loudly, with such gusto, she could be heard over the sound of late-evening traffic.

I spun around, turning my ear to the direction I'd heard the scream coming from as people began to disperse. Parents clung to their children's hands and Solomon had mine in a steel grip.

So I latched on to him and began to push my way through the crowd, coming to a dead halt when we reached the top of the stairs at the entry doors to the church.

There stood Carla Ratagucci, her eyes wide open in horror, her raven hair tousled from the wind with a hand over her mouth. My eyes followed her line of vision, and I fought not to follow her lead and put my hand over my mouth in horror, too.

In the doorway of the small storage closet at the rectory entry, there was a rolled-up tarp that blew with each slap of the wind as it whooshed in the doors.

When the wind blew the top of the tarp away, partially revealing the contents, I stopped short, my feet like lead.

It was a body.

But not just any body.

A headless body.

CHAPTER 7

I gripped Solomon's hand, pulling him closer to me to keep him near, and turning him to face the other direction, suddenly feeling quite exposed.

Spotting Coop a step or two down from the landing, trying to keep people from climbing the stairs to see the horror inside, I yelled her name as I made my way toward her. "Coop! Over here!"

In an instant, she was beside us, her glittering green eyes searching mine with a question. "Solomon? I want you to stay with Coop, okay? I'm going to go help Carla. Stay right near her, all right?"

Coop held out her hand to him, her eyes beseeching Solomon's, asking permission to touch him. "Solomon, will you take my hand, please?"

Solomon didn't blink once nor did he hesitate. Instead, he reached for Coop's hand and pulled it under his arm while I patted his shoulder and made a break back up the steps toward Carla.

She had her arms around her waist, almost doubled over

as though she were in pain, tears falling from her eyes in big wet splotches to the church's entryway floor as I reached for her.

"Carla!" I called, grabbing her by the arm and pulling her to me to shield her vision from the horrible sight.

"Oh, Trixie! It's—it's so *awful!*" she cried against my shoulder as I led her away from the closet and back outside toward Coop. Unfortunately, the crowd continued to grow as more and more people began to rubberneck the steps, climbing them with curious faces.

"Don't look," I ordered, turning her away from the sight. "Just keep walking toward Coop, okay?"

But she whimpered, stumbling over the slick hardwood, her heels wobbling. "I'll never get that out of my head, Trixie! How can I ever forget that?" she squealed, and it sounded like she was on the verge of hysteria.

Sister Patricia showed up out of nowhere, her face filled with distress, her hands reaching out for Carla, but Carla rebuffed her and turned away. Which was odd. Sister Patricia wasn't a favorite, by any means. She was rigid and inflexible, according to Sister O, but in a time of need, I'd think that would go by the wayside.

I didn't have much time to think about it before I saw the deacons. Deacon Delacorte stood tall in the throng of people gathering at the top step, his gorgeously angelic face racked with concern. "Miss Lavender?" he called to me in an emotion-choked voice, offering his hand to Carla. "Is that… is that what I think it is? Is he…or she…head…" He didn't finish the sentence due to what I'm sure amounted to his disbelief.

Deacon Cameron was directly behind him, his wrist over his mouth as he turned away, too.

"I don't know, but let me go and see if I can help, okay? Will you stay here with Carla, please? Coop? You, too. Just all of you stay together, and please call Tansy and Higgs," I instructed before I pivoted on my sneaker, tightened my sweater around me, and made my way toward the storage closet door.

There was no blood, no signs of a massacre, which one would think a crime scene like this would include when the end result was a beheading. The inside of the closet was lined with battery-operated candles, Bibles, and some boxes with no labels—tame compared to what lie on the floor at my feet.

What lie at my feet had to be addressed, and I was determined to investigate this like I would any other crime scene, gruesome or otherwise. On a deep breath, I sat on my haunches, keeping my hands in the pockets of my sweater so as not to contaminate.

The haze of the lights from above, soft and yellow, cast a far too gentle glow on what I was seeing, but I forced myself to scan the body and the surrounding areas.

My resolve lasted all of about two seconds before I had to stuff my fist in my mouth. I don't typically suffer from a weak stomach, but this...this headless body, so carelessly wrapped only in a tarp with some loose rope around it, had to mean something, didn't it?

Who would almost nonchalantly throw a body in a storage closet in a church? And was it connected to Sister Ophelia's murder?

And the nature of the crime was almost as upsetting as

the actual crime itself. Who would do something so horrible?

Yet, I forced myself to look, to absorb what I was seeing, to memorize the placement of the body, because I'd need that information later. Maybe I'd see a piece of evidence that triggered something—anything—that could help find who'd done this.

Was this related to Sister Ophelia's strangulation? And if it was related to Sister Ophelia, *how* was it related? It wasn't strangulation—or was it strangulation gone too far? My stomach rolled as though I was on a roller coaster ride, but I kept fighting the urge to vomit what little food I had in my stomach and persisted with my perusal of the crime scene.

I inched closer to the open door and peered down at the tarp, eyeing the body before inhaling deeply.

Details, Trixie. Focus on the details.

Whoever it was, I couldn't tell if it was male or female. However, if I had to make a semi-educated guess, I'd guess male. His thighs, bulging though the tarp, and the width and length of the body made me draw that conclusion.

His legs were longish, and what I could see of his shirt— a plaid flannel in red and blue—looked more like something a man would wear than a woman. Plus, the buttons to the shirt were on the right side, which typically indicated a male's shirt.

The tarp was thin, and certainly not at all sturdy. It looked more like a painting tarp used to cover a floor than one you'd use to wrap a body, and it appeared as though whoever had wrapped *this* particular body had done so in a hurry. There was no rhyme or reason to how it was covered or the way the rope was tied.

Which in and of itself was curious. But if you were going to dump a body—a headless body, no less—why would you dump it in, of all places, a church?

And the ugliest question of them all? Where the heck was the head that belonged to the body?

I looked up then, just as I heard Tansy and Co. rush up the stairs, the sound of their feet and the bark of orders comforting me.

"Trixie!" Tansy called to me as her officers moved inside en masse and began to shuffle everyone back out the church doors.

"Over here," I mumbled weakly, raising a hand in the air. I wanted to be strong. I really did, but I finally had to turn away from the body and inhale deeply before I gagged on what little saliva I had left.

The wind began to rush in through the doors as Tansy shouted orders to her people and I managed to keep from vomiting. When she finally approached me, her eyes were soft and sympathetic.

She propped an arm over my shoulder and patted and turned me away from the storage closet door, the bright lights of the interior of the church making my eyes water.

"Are you up to this, love? I feel like I've asked you that more'n once in the last two days, but this is particularly gruesome. I don't want you so upset you'll be ill."

I patted her hand and nodded, determined to do what I was here for—to help, to be of service.

"I think I am. As long as I can do it out there?" I asked, pointing to the doors of the church and the landing above the steps, where Carla stood with Coop and Solomon.

"So Carla found him...er, the body, eh? Poor love. She

must be all out of sorts. Will you come with so I can have a chat? Do you think you're up to it?"

"Of course. But let me warn you, she's beside herself."

"I can only imagine." Tansy nodded curtly at her men before shouting more orders as she steered me back outside into the rain. Oz saw us and instantly threw up an umbrella over our heads. I smiled my gratitude as I reached out for Carla's hand.

She let go of Coop and collapsed against me, her svelte body crumbling, her hands and arms trembling almost violently.

So I wrapped my arms around her and gave her a tight hug, hoping to calm her shudders. "It's all right, Carla. You're all right now. You're safe and the police are here. I'll stay with you every step of the way, okay?"

"*Please*," she whispered raggedly against my shoulder. "Please don't leave me, Trixie. It was so awful. I was just going to look for more candles and…and…"

Leaning back, I gripped her upper arms and nodded, brushing her hair from her eyes. "I understand. But I need you to give a statement to Tansy, okay? I'll stay with you the whole time, but it's really important if we want to catch whoever did this."

"I'll stay, too, Miss Ratagucci," Deacon Delacorte chimed in, his dark hair plastered to his skull from the rain. "As will Deacon Cameron."

Deacon Cameron, under a red and white umbrella himself, nodded briskly, looking out over the crowd of mourners. "Of course. Anything you need."

"Miss Ratagucci? I'm Tansy Primrose from Cobbler Cove PD. I'm so sorry for this misfortune, but I'd like a chat with you while it's all still fresh in your mind, yeah? Why don't we go inside where it's warm? I have word from Officer Meadows that Father Rico's been kind enough to offer his office to us."

Carla stiffened at the idea, but I patted her arms with reassurance. "I promise you won't even have to look in that direction, okay? I'll be right here."

"Okay," she whispered, her voice husky and gruff from crying.

As I led her back into the church, I steered her directly to the left and toward the long hallway leading to Father Rico's office door. I didn't want to see the crime scene any more than she did.

What I *did* want was to wrap my head around this tragedy enough to find some answers.

I just couldn't seem to get my feet under me.

~

*A*n hour later, sitting in Father Rico's office, we didn't have much more information than what had been obviously visible to even the most casual observer.

Father Rico's office was austere to say the least. He'd surrounded himself with burgundy curtains and stately rather than comfortable furniture. A dark-stained bookcase full of all sorts of tomes on Catholicism sat behind his large desk, with a lone reading lamp in gold on an end table near a corner chair. The décor was very different than the light and easygoing Father Rico.

As Carla sat in a stiff-backed chair, her legs tucked under the seat, her hands clenched together in a fist, she repeated herself once more in that shocked, monotone voice she'd adapted since we'd all sat down.

"I was just looking for more candles. I knew they were in the storage closet because when Sister Patricia called me to ask for help, I volunteered to hand them out to everyone in the first place. But we ran out..." she mumbled, her eyes filling with more tears.

I handed her another tissue and patted her leg. "So you didn't see anyone near the closet? No one at all? Not when you were helping Sister Patricia to organize the vigil? No one you didn't recognize?"

She shook her dark head, her hair now dry from the rain and curling around her pretty face in frizzy clumps. "*No!* I'm telling you, Trixie, when I went into that closet about two hours before the vigil, there was no one in there, or even around there. I knew everyone who helped Sister Patricia. There was nothing in that closet but...but...things that are *supposed* to be in a storage closet! I promise you, I'm telling the truth."

Tansy, leaning against the edge of Father Rico's enormous walnut-colored desk, licked her lips and scribbled on her pad. "So you needed more candles," she prompted.

"Yes. There were several latecomers. So I went to get more, and when I tried to open the storage closet door, I couldn't. I thought it was stuck. I swear, I thought it was only stuck!"

Tansy nodded. "And the door opens inward, yes?"

Carla looked at her, dark eyes swollen from crying, her lower lip trembling. "Yes. I don't know who designed the closets in this drafty tomb, but all the doors stick and push inward. Anyway, I pushed on it. I mean, I really gave it a good, hard shove with my shoulder. I guess," she paused and swallowed, running a hand through her hair, "I guess the... the body was holding the door shut or it was up against it and it fell or... *I don't know*. I just know it fell out and onto the floor right at my feet! That's all I know!"

Reaching out, I put my hand over Carla's tightly closed fist, her skin freezing cold to my touch. Both Tansy and I looked at each other, her eyes sending me the message that she'd gotten as much as she could from Carla.

We'd become pretty good at reading each other's facial expressions since we'd been working together, and it was clear this was all Carla could provide. She'd been stretched as thinly as possible and she needed a break.

Tansy dug into her soggy blazer and held out one of her business cards. "All right then, Miss Ratagucci. Let me give you my card and if you can think of anything else, anything at all, I'd be ever so grateful if you gave me a ring. If we need anything else from you, I'll let you know."

Rising from my chair, I held out my hand to Carla. "Let's get you home safe and sound, yes?"

Without a word, Carla rose on wobbly legs, taking my hand. When I opened the door to Father Rico's office, there was a small crowd of people waiting for us.

Higgs and Coop were there with Knuckles and Goose, and so were both of the deacons. Their faces all bleak with worry and lined with their weariness.

Knuckles gave me a hug and said against the top of my head, "You want me to take Carla home? Happy to do it if you need me to."

I turned in his embrace and asked Carla if she'd be all right with that. Her nod was silent, her movements sluggish as she let Knuckles herd her toward the door, leaving the rest of us to stare at each other in more shell-shocked silence, still in a state of disbelief.

Higgs was the first to speak when he said, "I'm stunned. I've seen a lot in my time on the force. I've seen a lot undercover, but I've never seen a killer be so careless. It's almost as if he wants to get caught."

Leaning back against the wall, I closed my eyes and nodded with a tired shake of my head. "There has to be something on the body to help us. Some fibers, a fingerprint —anything."

Goose leaned into me, giving me a nudge with his bony shoulder. "Speaking of fingerprints…"

I popped my eyes open and looked at him, head cocked. "What about them?"

Jamming his hands inside the pockets of his worn leather vest, he gave me a concerned gaze. "You sure you're ready for this?"

My shoulders slumped. "I'm as ready as I'll ever be. Lemme have it."

Moving closer to me, as the forensics team and police officers began to clear out, he said, "Whoever did this, Trixie girl, they didn't *just* chop off his head. I heard that forensics guy Pickles talkin' about it."

I fought a gasp and my weary legs began to tremble and I'm not sure if that was from fright or exhaustion, but I had to ask. "*What?*"

"You heard me, kiddo. This sicko didn't just cut his head off. They burned off his fingerprints, too."

CHAPTER 8

J was still trying to come to grips with the brutality of this particular murder as Coop and I entered our house—a place that had become my haven in all its soft hues and comfortable furniture.

Yet, I didn't feel as soothed by my surroundings as I normally did. My eyes were on fire and my legs were sore and shaky from tension. I knew I needed to sleep, I just didn't know how that was going to be possible.

I had no idea how I was ever going to get any rest tonight with the images of that body emblazoned in my brain. Add to that the idea that the corpse's fingerprints were burned off, and I couldn't shut my brain down for anything.

"Trixie Lavender? Would you like me to make you some chamomile tea to help you sleep?"

I plopped down on our couch and let my aching body sink into the deep cushions with a grateful sigh. The muted colors of the guest cottage we rented from Knuckles always brought me peace. His knack for decorating, for adding soothing warmth to a space, was most appreciated tonight.

Jeff hopped up next to me, tucking himself beside my thigh.

"Ya all right there, Trix?" he asked, putting his head in my lap and sighing.

We'd offered to bring him home with us so Higgs and Cal could settle the men at the shelter, who were quite uneasy, as a by the by. They weren't over their last run-in with a killer on the loose being so close to home. Adding another to the mix had left them nigh on paranoid, and who could blame them?

There was someone out there, killing nuns and throwing headless, fingerprint-less bodies into church storage closets with abandon. This wasn't a careful, methodical killer. He (and I use the pronoun loosely) was wandering around willy-nilly, and that was downright scary.

Still, I scratched Jeff's head, enjoying the warmth he provided. "I'm okay. Are *you* okay?"

"I did a whole lotta snoopin' around out there tonight, Trix. Listened in on a whole lotta conversations, heard pretty much nothin'. If the killer was there, he was careful."

"Well, at least he was careful about something. He sure isn't careful about leaving bodies lying around, is he?"

Livingston groaned from his perch. "Bodies, dumplin'? As in, now there's more'n one?"

Leaning my head back on the couch, I explained what had happened tonight with all the grim trimmings.

Livingston whistled long and low when I was through, spreading his wings. "Heavens to mergatroid," he muttered.

"Tell me about it. I mean, who dumps a body in the

storage closet of a church, for cripes' sake? Don't you find that a little bold?"

He scoffed and shuffled, his feathers rippling. "I'm still wonderin' who kills a sacred vessel of the Lord. I don't understand the motive for harmin' a harmless nun. I'm beginnin' to wonder if it has to do with somethin' she knew, Trixie. You keep sayin' the way she was snuffed out was done with vengeance, but who has hate for a nun 'cept for Satan himself?"

"Right?" I crowed, slapping my thigh. "What I really need to do is sit down with a pen and paper and hash this out in black and white. Your idea that this crime was motivated by something she knew makes perfect sense, and I need to hash that out. But for some reason, I haven't been able to get my feet under me since this thing started. Higgs says it's because I'm emotionally invested, and he's probably right. I'm not thinking with my head, but I'll need to if I'm ever going to catch who did this."

Coop returned with a steaming mug of tea and handed it to me, settling herself in the plump chair opposite the couch.

"I think it's best for all concerned if you get some sleep, Trixie. This day has been taxing enough without the added stress of murder boards and sticky notes."

I sipped at my tea and looked at her over the rim of my mug, letting the warm liquid slide down my throat. "I don't think I'll ever sleep again, Coop. I can't get the image of that body out of my head."

Nodding, Coop eyed me with her critical gaze, her raspy-smoky voice honest when she spoke. "It was pretty gruesome, but what good will you be if you don't get some rest? You can't go on with so little sleep. What help is that to Sister Ophelia?"

Ah, my Coop. Always the voice of reason. Jabbing a finger in the air, I agreed. "You're right. Maybe some of this yummy tea will help me relax enough to rest, and I'll wake up with all the answers to my questions about Sister Ophelia and the unidentified body in the storage closet." Or maybe I'd simply create more questions.

Coop pursed her lips and cocked her head to the left. "You know, speaking of the body, where do you suppose the killer left the head? It must be somewhere out there. Do you think the police will look for it? How would you even look for such a thing?"

Blanching, I fought a cringe as I leaned forward and set my half-empty mug on the coffee table. Death, even a brutal one like that of the headless body in the storage closet, didn't faze Coop in the way it did the rest of us. And that was through no fault of her own.

I had to remember she'd seen her fair share of horror, living in Hell for so long. She'd been witness to unspeakable horror, in fact. Seeing a beheaded body was probably akin to an afternoon stroll in hot lava before forty lashes with a whip.

Her matter-of-fact tone was simply her realism, poking its head through the muck of these murders.

"Good gracious, Coopie," Livingston chastised with a cluck of his tongue. "Don't be so crass, girl. 'Tis unseemly!"

"You hush, Quigley Livingston. I'm not being crass. I'm being practical, and practicality says the police will look for the head that belongs to the body. How else will they identify it? They don't even have fingerprints, so they'll need teeth to try to match with dental records."

Coop, schooled in the college of *Law & Order: SVU* and *CSI*, had obviously learned a thing or two about what came next in an instance such as this.

"She's right, Livingston. Though, I don't know how they'll do it or where they'll even begin. If the two murders are tied together, I don't know what the common thread could be, but whoever murdered the person in the storage closet doesn't want them to be identified. Yet, I can't help but wonder, is this even related to Sister O's death at all?"

"Two murders at a church are certainly not a coincidence, Trixie Lavender."

"Okay, so let's look at the method of murder. Sister Ophelia was strangled. The body was beheaded. Was the body strangled, too?"

"Strangulation is an angry act, Trix. Real angry," Jeff chimed in. "I saw a news report on it when Higgs was watching *Dateline*."

"Okay, so what's a beheading if not angry, right?" I shook my head and sipped more of my tea. "None of this is making any sense. But right now, my priority is Sister Ophelia's murder—at least until we find out who the body belongs to and if they're connected in some way."

Coop crossed her slender legs, leaning forward to stroke Jeff's spine. "So tomorrow, after you've had a fortifying night of sleep, we'll sit down and do what we always do. We'll start with social media, we'll look at all the parties involved and see what they're posting, who they know. You know, the usual, and then branch out from there."

"I have a feeling social media isn't going to be much help,

Coop. I mean, we're talking nuns here. At least in Sister Ophelia's case, there won't be much to find. They're people of faith. They don't use social media the way we do. Facebook is more like a global bulletin board for them rather than a way to socialize."

"That's probably true, but maybe someone who *does* use social media on the reg posted on one of their pages. And after we do all that, we talk to people, right? Deacon Delacorte was one of the last people to talk to Sister Ophelia. He's a start. Then we move on to Deacon Cameron and Sister Patricia and so on."

I loved Coop's optimism, especially when I lacked any right now. That and focus. I was having trouble staying the course. I should have talked to those people before I ever left the church the night the sister was murdered, and if not then at least the next day. Though, I wasn't sure exactly what more they could tell me that hadn't already been told.

Still, it wasn't like me at all.

"Yes," I confirmed tiredly. "We can definitely do those things, Coop. But my hope is Tansy will have more information tomorrow once this new body's seen the coroner's eyes. Maybe whatever they used to kill Sister Ophelia was what they used to kill the person in the storage closet, and we'll have some kind of evidence to help us."

Coop took my empty mug from me and set it on the wood coffee table. "I think for now, you should call it a night and get some rest. At least try to sleep. I don't have any appointments until late afternoon. So I can help you in the morning." She held out her hand to me. "C'mon. Bedtime."

I didn't refuse her because protesting was futile. Not to

mention, I needed some time alone to process what was happening and find a way to come to terms with the images burned in my brain.

Grabbing her hand, I dropped a kiss on Livingston's head and plodded toward my bedroom with Jeff in tow. "Thanks, Coop. you were awesome tonight with Solomon. I appreciate you and everything you do."

She glared at me before pulling up either side of her mouth with her fingers, making a smile. "I'm always happy to help. Even if you can't see it on my face."

I giggled before I gave her a quick hug and whispered, "I'll see you in the morning. Make sure you fire up your laptop so we can social-media stalk our very few suspects."

She gave me the thumbs-up sign. "You bet. Wake me if you need me."

I closed the door and let the silence of my bedroom permeate my ears. Jeff slid silently to the far side of the bed and situated himself in his usual place of rest on a set of cushiony pillows, while I headed in to wash my face and brush my teeth.

As I ran a quick brush over my hair, I ignored the deep shadows under my eyes and the pinched look on my pale face. All I wanted to do was block out the night's events and attempt some sleep. I padded to the edge of my bed and pulled down the fluffy comforter, not even bothering to remove the throw pillows Knuckles had so painstakingly chosen.

Crawling into bed, I clicked the light off and stretched from head to toe before rolling to my side and staring off at the wall, watching the reflection of the lights dance from outside on our small patio.

I reached out a hand and stroked Jeff's back, the wiry texture of his fur soothing me. The last thing I remember before the bliss of sleep overtook was Sister O's face, smiling at me as she told me about the last episode of *Perry Mason* she'd watched. She loved Perry Mason almost as much as I loved Monk and Jessica Fletcher.

Clinging to that image, I drifted off to sleep.

~

"*T*rixie! Wake up!"

I felt the bed sag and ripple beneath me and heard Jeff's voice from somewhere far off.

"Coop! Coop, get in here now! Trixie's havin' a wicked nightmare! *Cooop!*"

I fought to open my eyes, but it felt as though they were glued shut. So I jolted upward, my body pitching forward, only to crash to the floor and knock my head on the corner edge of my nightstand.

I managed to force my eyes open, holding up my hands to thwart Jeff, who was inches from my face, his hot breath whooshing under my nose.

Then Jeff was on top of me, pawing my arm, seconds before Coop burst in looking fresh as a daisy. "Trixie? Trixie, what happened?"

I scooted up and pressed my back against the nightstand. "I don't know," I grumbled, my throat sore and dry.

"She was doin' that thing again, Coopie!" Jeff declared, his body shaking, his tone anxious as he danced from foot to foot. "Drawin' on her sketch pad like her fingers didn't belong to her. She was drawin' and rockin' and it was wicked bananas! I tried to wake her up, but she couldn't hear me."

I placed my hands on either side of my body and hauled myself upward, wobbling when I was fully erect. Coop had switched on the light, giving me a clear glimpse of the mess I'd made. Pillows were on the floor, the comforter rumpled and shoved to one side, and there in the middle of it all was my sketch pad.

The vanilla paper, covered in my pencil strokes, loomed in front of me. I reached for it, my hands shaking as I tried to clear the cobwebs in my head and focus on what I'd sketched.

"How odd," Coop said from over my shoulder.

And I had to agree. How odd indeed.

"If you think *that's* odd, you shoulda seen her drawin' it," Jeff exclaimed, hopping up on the bed and dancing around. "She was sketchin' like her life depended on it, but her eyes weren't even open!"

Ah. So evidently, Artur was back, and back with a vengeance. The last time I'd done something like this was when Dr. Mickey had been killed, and the sketch I'd drawn —or should I say, Artur had drawn—had been a clue. We didn't understand it at the time, but it all made sense once Dr. Mickey's murder had been solved.

This time, I planned to pay closer attention.

It's not like I had anything reliable to go on. This phenomenon had only happened once. Could I even trust it was a clue?

"Artur?" I murmured to Coop as I craned my neck to look at her.

She blinked and shook her head. "I don't understand. If

we consider what little information we have on the demon inside you, he apparently helped us the last time you did this. Remember?"

Nodding, I rubbed my eyes, realizing for the first time it was morning and, while the sun wasn't exactly shining, it was certainly light out.

"I do. How could I forget?"

"So if he's evil, why did he help you last time, even if we didn't realize he was helping, and what does *this* mean?" She held up the sketch and I examined it more closely.

"I don't get it either," I whispered, my words shaky.

Yet, my drawing was very clear. In fact, if Artur was the one responsible for this, he was pretty good—far better at shading than I'd ever be.

Coop scratched her head, pushing her long dusky-red hair over her shoulder. "It's just a picture of a television."

It sure was. And that was *all* it was—a picture of a TV with nothing on the screen. How bizarre.

I looked to Coop, feeling ridiculously helpless. "I don't understand. Is this a clue like the last time? Does this mean I should watch the TV? Or do you think it has something to do with Sister Ophelia and the headless corpse?"

"We only have the prior time you've done this to go on, and back then it turned out to be a clue. One we didn't understand, but a clue regardless. I think that's the angle we should take, Trixie Lavender."

I ran a hand through my hair, sighing a ragged breath. "Okay, that aside, why is he showing up after all this time?"

Jeff suddenly dropped to his haunches and cocked his head. "You know, you guys are always wicked bangin' on this demon in Trixie, but did ya ever consider he might be one of the good ones? Like Coop? She's not a bad demon. Neither am I."

Huh. I hadn't thought about that side of the coin. Not even once. But… "If this thing in me's so good, why did it moon the sisters at the convent, and why does it rage the way it does? It turns me into a monster, Jeff."

"You say monster, I say misguided," he joked. "Maybe we're goin' about this all wrong."

I held up a hand as my phone buzzed with the sound of a text. "Maybe we are, but I have my doubts. Still, let's table that discussion and figure out who murdered Sister O. Artur and his shenanigans can wait."

Glancing down at my phone on the nightstand, I cocked my head. It was from someone anonymous.

I have information about Sister Ophelia's murder to share with you. Meet me at Our Lady at two p.m. today. I'll be in the confessional. Leave your phone on the altar and come alone. If you alert the police, I'll know.

CHAPTER 9

"Okay, so here's what I've got so far. You guys with me?" I asked Coop, Livingston, and Jeff as I pointed to my notes.

"Roight there wit ya, Miss Marple," Livingston teased, his glassy eyes widening as he pecked at some raspberry pastries Knuckles had dropped off before leaving to open Inkerbelle's.

I narrowed my gaze at him and shook a finger. "Don't you start, too, Funny Man." Rubbing my hands together, I spread out my notes on our dining room table and fought a yawn.

I guess I'd really slept last night, because the aftereffects felt a bit like a hangover, even after a shower. I had a meeting with an unknown person at two and the curiosity was killing me. To keep my mind busy, I decided to jot down some notes and do as Coop suggested while she scanned some Facebook pages.

Most of which brought us nothing of value. But sometimes, talking it out aloud helped. Pointing to the lined paper, I looked over what I'd scribbled.

"So, here's our timeline. Sister O was strangled to death, right? She'd gone out to smoke a cigarette. She was obviously stressed about something. Or at least she said that's typically when she smokes—in times of stress."

"Yes, and shortly before she went out to smoke, she told Father Rico she needed to speak with him," Coop chimed in as she leaned forward, putting her elbows on the table.

"But before that, she had a run-in with Daniel Coletti, where he threatened to kill her about a failing grade."

Coop cracked her knuckles and settled into her chair. "But he has a solid alibi, according to Tansy. He's off the table. That brings us back to Father Rico."

"Right. But we don't know what Sister O wanted to talk to him about because Father Rico was preparing to kick off the speed-dating event and he cut her short."

Coop held up a finger to interrupt. "Speaking of the speed-dating event, may I ask a question that's been puzzling me since that night?"

Crossing my arms over my chest, I nodded. "Of course, Coop."

"I'd forgotten all about this until you mentioned the speed dating. What exactly does 'can I follow you? Because my mother told me to follow my dreams' mean?"

Both Livingston and I looked at Coop with blank stares. "Whatever are ya goin' on about, Coopie? What kind of nonsense gobbledygook is that?"

She pursed her lips. "Someone said those words to me at the speed-dating event. Someone else said, 'Kissing burns five calories a minute. How about a workout?'"

Both Livingston and I laughed out loud, and Jeff, at Coop's feet, snorted.

"That's called a pickup line, Coop. Someone was trying to pick you up," I informed her, patting her hand with a grin.

She sat up straight, her beautiful face contorting. "Pick me up? No one tried to pick me up, Trixie Lavender, and I wouldn't have let them had they tried. Besides, I'm probably too heavy for most of the men I met to pick up."

Now we laughed even harder as I shook my head. "No, Coop. Not *literally* pick your body up—"

"Oh, I dunno, lass. In Coopie's case, I think that's exactly what that means!" And then Livingston laughed harder.

Coop eyed us with one of her infamous dead stares coupled with some icy daggers on the side. "I don't know if you can tell from my face, but I am *not* amused. I'm asking a genuine question about you humans and you're mocking me."

Which only made us laugh harder.

When I finally caught my breath, I had to wipe the tears from my eyes. "No, Coop. I promise I'm not mocking you. Your innocence is a breath of fresh air, but sometimes it catches me off guard. Now, when I say they were trying to pick you up, I mean they were using their words in the hopes you'd find them clever enough to want to date them. Lines like, 'Are you lost? Because Heaven is a long way from here' implies you're an angel and you fell from Heaven. It's mostly a compliment, if not a really cheesy one."

Coop looked affronted, maybe even offended. "That's ridiculous. Angels don't fall from Heaven. They do something bad and get kicked out."

I bobbed my head, my eyes returning to my notes. I didn't want to know how she knew that specific detail

"Yep. Definitely a discussion for another time."

"You always say that," she replied, rolling her eyes the way she'd seen Brenda do in reruns of *90210*. That was her latest binging passion, and she loved Brenda.

"And you always impart a new detail about your supernaturalness, and the backstory's always something I'm not sure I'm quite prepared to hear. But we can go into greater depth about the speed dating later if you need to. In the meantime, let's move on, okay?" Clearing my throat, I swallowed another giggle. "So where were we?"

"Speed datin', Coop style," Jeff said on a laugh, rolling to his back.

"Right. Okay, so after Sister Ophelia told Father Rico she needed to speak with him, she went out to smoke. But we're forgetting the conversation Sister Ann overheard in the closet at the school. That happened a couple of days before her death and before the event. From the sounds of it, someone was confessing an affair to Sister O because she caught her in the act and it was quite possibly another nun. But apparently, Sister O made it clear to this person she should fess up. So that's certainly motive for murder, right?"

"But 'twould a nun resort to murder, Trixie?" Livingston squawked. "I'm havin' trouble reconcilin' that and attributin' it to a vessel of the Lord."

"Anyone is capable of murder, Livingston," Coop assured us. "Believe me when I tell you, there have been many men of the cloth in Hell."

"You just love to shatter a good illusion, don't ya, lass?"

Coop shrugged her slender shoulders and fiddled with the strings on her hoodie. "I only speak the truth."

"Okay," I intervened. "Vessels of the Lord in Hell aside, we have one suspect. Whoever talked to Sister Ophelia in the coat closet at the school."

"Yes, but if we've come to the conclusion that vessels of the Lord are capable of murder, how can we know for sure Sister Ann was telling you and Higgs the truth? Maybe no one ever confessed anything to Sister Ophelia, and she's simply trying to keep us off her scent because she's the one who murdered the sister?"

I groaned and put my head in my hands, rubbing my temples with my thumbs. "That would throw a hitch in our giddyup, for sure. I think we have to stick with the facts for now and not look for plot twists just yet. Let's wait on the Sister Ann angle until we can find something that points us in her direction."

"Then that brings us to last night and the body in the storage closet," Coop reminded, her face even more grim than normal.

Nodding, I grabbed my phone, vibrating with an incoming text from Tansy. As I read, I sighed. Ugh.

"Trixie? What's happening?"

"I just got a text from Tansy and the preliminary reports from the coroner are not a match between the two bodies in terms of the method of death. Meaning yes, Sister Ophelia was strangled, but they're not sure with what yet. Tansy says she has some feelers out about what was used, but she didn't say where or why, and I'm not going to ask because she won't tell me until she's good and ready anyway. Plus, I'm not that desperate *yet*.

However, headless guy is definitely a guy, and he wasn't strangled at all. His head was definitely removed by something sharp."

Livingston shivered. "How dreadful for the poor chap."

So dreadful I couldn't dwell on it or I'd lose my breakfast. Instead, I decided to ask her for permission to search Sister Ophelia's room. I really needed to see if she had a TV that looked like what I'd sketched. But my phone remained silent.

That meant I needed to keep moving until I heard from her. "Coop, anything interesting on Facebook or Twitter? Maybe Instagram?"

Instagram was a long shot. I mean, how many nuns do you know who take pictures of their bologna and cheese sandwiches (which is a typical lunch, by the way), or their day trips spent frolicking at the beach in their string bikinis? Pretty much none, I'd suppose. But stranger things have been known to happen, right?

Coop shook her head. "Nothing of great note. Sister Ophelia didn't have any social media to speak of. In fact, none of the nuns involved have pages on Facebook or Twitter, but the church has a page. There were plenty of condolences for her, and they dedicated a lovely post to her, too. I combed the comments, but I didn't find anything of note. Definitely nothing out of the ordinary."

I tapped my pen on the paper then circled Father Rico's name. "Which brings me to Father Rico. Tansy told me he had a pretty harrowing experience before he became a priest."

Coop frowned, her eyebrows mashing together. "You don't think Father Rico's a suspect, do you, Trixie? I'd be devastated. I so enjoy his sermons." She paused and heaved a long sigh. "Gosh, I really don't want it to be Father Rico."

I sent her a sympathetic smile. "I know, Coop. I'm not ruling anyone out if we go on our vessels-of-the-Lord theory, but I don't really think he's a suspect. However, when I tell you what happened to him, I have to wonder if someone from his past could be involved. It's a pretty slim chance, but I'm not taking anything off the table."

I explained Father Rico's gas station experience when he was taken hostage while I gathered up our now cold coffee cups and set them in the sink. Coop helped me clean up from breakfast, listening intently.

When I was done, she turned the dishwasher on and folded the kitchen towel. "Poor Father Rico. I wonder if he's told anyone about it? If he's ever shared it with maybe Higgs? They are friends, after all."

Grabbing my purse, I stuffed my phone into it and dug around for the keys to our beat-up Caddy. "I plan to ask him just that when I talk to deacons Cameron and Delacorte today. I'm also going to see if I can't take a peek in Sister O's room. I know the police have gone through it, but I'd like to see it for myself. After that, I'm going to check out the alleyway and maybe talk to some of the parishioners I know who attended the event."

"Well, one thing's for sure, you're not going into that confessional alone," Coop said, a warning in her tone. "I'm going with you."

Coop was right. I shouldn't go alone. Whoever this was, they'd picked a time when the church was virtually empty. Father Rico left for lunch at one-thirty every day like clockwork, and afternoon mass didn't begin until three. All the nuns were off doing their due diligence either at the school or through community work. Likely, the only person about would be Leland, the janitor.

Whoever this was with the important information about Sister O, it was someone who knew the church schedule.

"While I'll definitely feel safer with you there, we're going to have to find a way to hide you, because I can't afford to miss this opportunity. I don't want whoever it is to be spooked. What if this person really has something important to share that could help with the investigation?"

Coop gave me a pointed look. "Why wouldn't they share it in person instead of hiding behind a confessional?"

"Maybe they're afraid?"

But of what? Or who? Did Sister Ophelia have some storied past we weren't aware of? A zillion questions flew through my mind, leaving me more confused than ever.

"Of what, Trixie? Of the killer? If they know who the killer is, they'd just turn him in, wouldn't they? That likely means they have information about something suspicious but nothing definitive. Why wouldn't they want that information out in the open? I don't trust this person. I have a bad feeling right here." She pointed to the pit of her flat stomach. "So I'm coming and that's that, and I'll hear no argument from you. I'll figure out where to hide before they get there, but you're not going alone. Now let's go to the shop and see if Goose and Knuckles need anything."

A well of admiration sprung up from my gut for Coop. Every day, she made a new stride of some kind or another, and it never failed to make the mother hen in me crow my pride.

Turning to Livingston, I asked, "Are you up to seeing

your fan club today, Mr. Charisma? Or would you prefer to stay in and rest on your laurels?"

Livingston had created quite a stir with not only our customers, but our neighboring business owners. People loved him. In fact, aside from the gorgeous tattoo artist who never smiled, Livingston was one of Inkerbelle's biggest draws, and he ate it up like he guzzled down a plate of spaghetti—even if it did leave his owl tummy in gassy distress.

He flapped a wing at us. The gray and tan of his freshly washed feathers glistening in the weak sunlight pouring in from the bay of kitchen windows.

"I'm takin' the day off, lass. My adoring fans shall have to wait until I'm up to cavortin'."

I dropped a kiss on his head and chuckled before I put Jeff's leash around his neck and we headed out, my stomach in a knot about my upcoming meeting.

Still, I sent out a prayer to the universe that this information from this anonymous source would lead to something substantial. Because otherwise, we were on a fast train to nowhere.

⁓

I entered the church at two sharp with my heart in my throat and my stomach on full tilt. I had no idea what I was in for, or what I was about to hear, but I was as tense as an arrow poised on a bow.

Coop had snuck in through the window of Father Rico's office to avoid being seen. I hated not telling him what we were about to do, but I hated even more the idea of losing this person with alleged information to fear, and possibly making them flee. Coop hid up in the balcony area by way of the stairs from the back of the church, her movements stealthy and sure and eerily quiet.

Taking a deep breath, I made my way down the aisle and, out of pure instinct, formed the sign of the cross as I neared the altar. Then I held up my phone to the empty space to show I was doing as asked and set it down on the altar's steps.

Lighted candles lined the stairs to the pulpit and the heavy cross hanging above it loomed over me, making my heart clamor in my chest.

I already felt deceptive enough for not telling Father Rico or Higgs or anyone else what I was doing. I didn't need the added pressure and guilt of the Big Guy.

The weak sunlight at the beginning of the day had waned, and as I looked out through the beauty of the arched stained-glass windows, I noticed it had gone gloomy and had begun to rain, mirroring my internal feelings.

I slipped inside the heavy wood confessional off to the far left of the altar, wondering if the person who'd sent the text was already inside waiting for me as I settled in.

When I heard the screen for the confessional slide open, my head popped up and I squinted into the small, dark space, but I could only see an outline of a head, and it appeared to be covered by a hood.

"Is this the part where you say, 'Forgive me, Father, for I have sinned'?" I joked out of nervousness.

"What they say is true. I heard you were funny," a voice whispered, a quiet voice that had an added almost hiss on the letter "S".

Wiping my hands on my thighs, I fought to remain calm —to *sound* like I was calm. This person knew me, and that was a little frightening.

"Did you then? So you know me?"

"I know *of* you, Trixie," the voice rasped, his words sliding into my ears, making the hair on the back of my neck stand on end.

"Okay, well, since you know my name, how shall I address you?"

He cleared his throat. At least the voice sounded like a male. "You don't have to address me at all. You just have to listen."

Now he was sounding a bit more commanding. So I decided to take an easygoing approach.

"Can I ask you a couple of questions first?"

His reply was stiff and probably said through clenched teeth. "Ask, and I'll decide if I answer."

Strangely, he didn't sound at all antagonistic, but he definitely sounded agitated. Yet I wasn't sure if his agitation had to do with fear or aggravation.

"Why didn't you text me this information if you didn't want to reveal your identity? Why all the cloak-and-dagger stuff? In fact, why a real-time meeting at all?"

His laughter wisped into the void of the confessional. "I'm terrible at technology. If I were to try to text you what I know, we'd be here until next year."

I cocked my head in confusion. "Why not just call me then?"

"Because I don't want my phone call traced to my location or, worse, to me. So I bought a throwaway phone and got your phone number from the church rectory."

I couldn't help but laugh a little at the absurdity of that statement. "I don't know the first thing about tracing your location. You can trust that's not my expertise. Not to mention, you could have just called me on your burner cell, it's likely untraceable anyway. That's why they're for."

"But you *do* know the police," he reminded, his voice even stronger now. "In fact, you work with them on a regular basis. It wouldn't be so hard for you to find the means to trace my whereabouts. How do I know how advanced technology's become? Maybe they can trace burner cells now."

I guess that was true, but I wasn't sure of the finer details involved, and I couldn't help but point out how paranoid that sounded. What the heck was he going to tell me anyway?

"It sounds like you watch a lot of TV. I'm not sure if that's even possible."

"Whether it's true or not isn't the point. I'm simply taking every precaution. I can't afford to be caught. I have…" He cleared his throat again. "Let's just say, I have a history with the police."

So I was talking to a criminal? I was ever so glad Coop was waiting in the wings. "So you're telling me you're a criminal?"

He sighed, letting out some of what I figured was frustration. "Not exactly. Not anymore, but I don't want anything to do with the cops. *Period.*"

"Okay, so why meet here—in the church?"

"Because it's sacred. You're an ex-nun. You know what that means to someone of faith. The confessional is confidential."

Now we were getting somewhere. I folded my hands together and inhaled. "Are you someone of faith? Because I'm not a priest. Whatever you tell me isn't confidential. I'm an ex-nun, as you said, and in the scheme of things, that means nothing."

I heard the person shift in their seat, likely in discomfort. "The confessional gives me a certain amount of anonymity while still allowing me to unload in person. But that doesn't matter. Never mind who I am and why I chose the church as a meeting place," he said briskly. "All you need to know is, I came in good faith to share something I know that could help you with Sister Ophelia's murder. I just want to help without all the messy involvements the cops bring, okay? I'm just trying to do the right thing."

Now he was getting agitated, and I didn't want to anger him enough to incite him into leaving. Some pacification was in order.

"I get it, and I appreciate the effort you made."

"Good. Now, when I'm done, I'm going to ask you to count to one hundred while I slip out of here, and I want no further involvement in this disgusting mess. Understood?"

Wow. He'd whipped through a range of emotions. Anxious, paranoid, and now demanding. But I was willing to do what I had to in order to get the information I needed.

"Understood," I said, but I heard my voice waver, and he picked up on that.

"You don't sound sure—but I am. If you can't give me your word you won't follow me and reveal who I am, I won't tell you anything. You being an ex-nun should at least mean you're good for your word."

I hated giving my word about things of this nature,

THE SMOKING NUN

because someone could end up hurt if I didn't reveal my
source, but I was going to do it in light of the greater good.
"You have my word. Now, please tell me what you know."

There was an excruciatingly long pause, which I'm sure
amounted to no more than two seconds but felt like two
years.

"I think I know who killed Sister Ophelia."

I'd believe it when I heard it. "And who do you think
killed Sister Ophelia?"

"Sister Patricia Latimer."

CHAPTER 10

It took all of my will not to gasp out loud while I clutched my pearls in shock. Sister Patricia? Staid, rigid, sourpuss Sister Patricia was a murderer? Well, knock me over with a feather.

As I digested that information, I let out a slow breath and asked, "And how do you know this?"

"I heard her arguing with Sister Ophelia on Friday in the coat closet at the school."

I blinked in my shock. No one else knew about that conversation but myself, Tansy, Higgs, and Sister Ann—or at least as far as I knew. That meant the information was at least legit.

That also meant this was someone from the school or familiar with the school. Golly, there were plenty of men who worked at Our Lady. It could be anyone from a priest to a janitor.

"And before you go deducing things, I don't work at the school. I was only there on an errand, and I overheard the conversation. You couldn't help but overhear it."

Hear that? That was my theory flying directly out the window on the wings of disillusion. Dang it all.

As he talked, his voice became stronger, as though he were getting something off his chest he could no longer live with.

"So what exactly did you hear?"

"I heard Sister Patricia confirm Sister Ophelia's suspicions that she was having an affair with the parent of a student. I heard her say it loud and clear."

My heart began to pound inside my chest to beat the band. That was some sticky information. But hello. Sister Patricia—and I repeat, *staid, rigid, sourpuss* Sister Patricia—was having a torrid affair? I think if you'd told me the apocalypse was started by a bunch of kindergartners, I'd have been more likely to believe you than to believe Sister Patricia was breaking her vows so outrageously.

I had to hold on to the edge of my seat to keep myself upright, but I still managed to ask, "Okay, did she say who the parent was?"

He barked a cynical laugh. "No. Of course she didn't, but Sister Ophelia sounded like she knew. She said she saw them. If you ask me, Sister Patricia was relieved to unload and dump the burden on someone else just to get it off her chest."

Well, wasn't that what confessing a sin was all about anyway? Confessing any wrongdoing was about unburdening yourself, seeking absolution.

Also, there was no love lost between Sister O and Sister Patricia. They'd rubbed each other the wrong way. So I wondered why she'd confess something of such a sensitive nature even though Sister Ann claimed Sister O did say she *saw them.* This mystery man's statement cleared that up. She'd been caught. That's why she'd confessed. Sister O must have been in the process of confronting her.

"And what did Sister Ophelia tell her? Did she tell her she'd have to share this with the hierarchy? Or did she promise to keep Sister Patricia's secret?"

"She told her she'd made a vow to God to be faithful, and she'd broken her commitment to Him."

Basically he was telling me the same thing Sister Ann relayed to us. Whoever this was, he wasn't lying. Next, I asked the dreaded question—one I almost didn't want to hear the answer to.

"Did she threaten Sister Ophelia in any way?"

"No. But she did beg her not to tell anyone. Still, Sister Ophelia wouldn't hear of it. She said Sister Patricia knew she was morally obligated to tell Father Rico if she was aware of a nun committing a sin. She also said it was unfair that the sister asked her to keep a confidence when it was such an enormous infraction. She called it an albatross, and she urged Sister Patricia to talk to Father Rico so she wouldn't have to."

Well, that definitely was a motive for murder for some, but a *nun?* I still wasn't so sure. Sister Patricia was already breaking a bunch of commandments just by having the affair. To kill someone over it was taking a step off the edge of the cliff and falling into the abyss.

Although, I'll say it once more for the people in the back, I wouldn't put murder past *anyone.* Not after what I've seen.

That led me to wonder, would Sister O really have tattled on her? I couldn't be sure. I'd only known her for two months. But I had to pause and wonder if even I would tell. It was such a slap in the face to her vows, but would I have had the guts to out someone if I were in Sister O's position?

"How do you know for sure it was Sister Patricia and Sister Ophelia in the coat closet? Are you one hundred percent sure it was them?"

"*Because I saw them*," he said with what almost sounded like disdain. "I know who they are, Trixie. I see them all the time. There was another nun who ran away before they came out, too. I think it was Sister Ann. I bet she heard them. You should ask her what *she* heard. She'll verify what I'm telling you."

Another bit of information, confirming what Sister Ann had told us. Also, he was familiar with the staff at the school. Did that mean he was a parent? Delivery person? Was there a camera by the coat closet? I'd have to ask Tansy to check.

I decided to fish in the deep end of the pond in the hopes I'd get him to tell me who he was.

"So no one else saw you at the school that day?"

There was some agitated movement and a shuffle of his feet, before he said, "I don't know what you're fishing for, but you're not going to get it out of me. You don't need to know who I am because I had *nothing* to do with this. I heard something I wish I hadn't, and I battled with myself about whether to tell anyone. My conscience won. The police were out of the question, so you were the next best thing. Don't make me sorry. So, for the last time, this is all I know. Sister Patricia had an affair with a student's father. She confessed it to Sister Ophelia after confronted. Sister Ophelia said she was going to be forced to tell Father Rico. I don't know if the man is married, nor do I have any more information than what I've told you."

If he wasn't going to reveal himself, there really wasn't much more to say, was there?

Sighing, I made another executive decision not to push and scare him off. "Fair enough. But if you remember anything else, if you hear something, anything, will you text me again, please?"

"Yeah," he drawled. "Sure."

And then the "fixer" in me couldn't help but take inventory on this man who sounded so disillusioned.

"Can I ask you one last question?"

"Hurry it up. I have to get out of here."

"When you spoke of the nuns, you sounded angry. May I ask why?"

I don't know why I cared or even why I asked, but there were moments when he spoke that he'd sounded lost, and that, in turn, spoke to me in a way I can't describe.

His soft bark of laughter dripped with scorn. "Oh, believe me, I don't think I can even define the half of it in words. Suffice to say, your God left me a long time ago, or maybe I left him when he abandoned me. I don't know. The point is, you're all a bunch of hypocrites anyway. I think I've proven that just by what I've told you about Sister Patricia and her little fling, haven't I?"

Without a doubt, this man was angry and hurt, but my gut told me he wasn't a bad person. However, he did have some kind of grudge and he was lashing out. I wanted to understand why.

I held up my hands as if he could see them, using them as white flags of surrender. "You're absolutely right. What

Sister Patricia did is very hypocritical. But even the holy stumble and fall. I'm sorry that somewhere along the way, something happened that left you feeling this way. But I want you to know, I understand where you're at. I'm not an ex-nun for nothing. I've felt disappointment with my faith, too. But if you ever want to talk to someone—someone like me, who won't judge you or try to talk you into coming back to the church, you can text me. I'd be happy to simply listen."

I wanted him to understand that even though I was no longer a nun, I hadn't shunned my faith entirely because it had failed me. I knew exactly where he was coming from with his feelings of hypocrisy.

After what happened to me the night I was possessed, no one had given me the second chance our faith touts. No one had even considered that.

Yet, it didn't stop me from believing the idea of God, whether real or imagined, was designed to spread good. I wanted this man to know you didn't have to be bitter because you were at odds with your faith.

There were other ways to find your own path, and being so angry could only lead to an eventual self-destruction. I wanted him to see that there could still be so much joy and happiness to be found if you only looked.

He was silent for a time, and I decided to let him sit with my words instead of push.

When he sighed, I heard the defeat as he exhaled. He sounded like someone who'd been on a long journey, and it was well past time to rest his weary mind.

"You know, that's the first time someone who's even remotely involved with the church has said something like that to me instead of quoting me Bible verses and telling me I needed to find my way back to the flock. Thank you, Trixie. Maybe when this is all over, I might do that. Until then, I hope you find the killer—for Sister Ophelia's sake and for yours."

That was my fervent hope, too. "Thank you," I whispered. "Shall I begin counting to one hundred now?"

He laughed, but this time it was lighter and not nearly as tight and intense. "Please."

As I counted out loud so he knew I wasn't cheating, I heard the shuffle of feet, the push of the curtain opening, and then footsteps as they faded and the door to the vestibule opened and shut.

Then there was a knock on the confessional door that made me jump. "It's safe, Trixie."

I popped the door open. "Coop? How did you get down here so freakishly fast?"

She glared at me with her ultra-serious gaze. "Demon magic," she said flatly as she peered at me.

Chuckling, I went to grab my phone from the altar and hit the bricks. I had some questions to ask and Sister Ophelia's room to sift through.

"Did you see anything?"

"No. And he definitely doesn't want to be seen. He had on a ski mask *and* a hoodie."

"Anything identifying? Maybe he walks with a limp?"

But Coop shook her head, the cascade of her auburn hair floating about her back. "No. Though he was quite tall," she said as we passed a pillar at the end of the aisle. She held her hand up to it and marked a spot. "He came to about here. I'd say he's over six feet."

I sighed. Not that it truly mattered what he looked like, I suppose. I was almost more curious about why he couldn't reveal himself to me than I was his confirmation of Sister Ann's story. The one thing I didn't feel was suspicion. He was a man tormented by something who was doing the right thing despite his misgivings about the law and the Lord. I felt that in my gut.

"I felt sorry for him, Coop. Did you hear how defeated he sounded?"

"You're losing your objectivity again, Trixie Lavender. This isn't about the man in the confessional. This is about finding a killer."

I patted her on the back. "You're right, but that doesn't mean I can't care about a fellow human being and his pain."

"Is this one of your teachable moments?"

I smirked at her and rolled my eyes. "This is one of my multitasking moments—look for Sister O's killer and be concerned about a fellow human being who's hurting. I don't know what went so wrong for him, but I felt a connection to him just the same. I get what he's feeling because to a degree, I've felt it, too."

"I just want you to stay focused on what we set out to do, Trixie Lavender. Find Sister Ophelia's killer."

"I can do both things at once, Coop." Brushing my hands together as we approached the door, I decided we needed to get down to the business of asking some questions. "So mystery man aside, are you ready to ask some questions with me? I need to get into Sister Ophelia's room and see if the TV I drew is in there."

"Where does she live anyway? I've never seen a convent in Portland, so I wondered."

"She lives...*lived* in a church owned building. Co-owned, actually. By both St. Andrews and Our Lady. So the nuns all have their own bedrooms and bathrooms and then there are common areas like the kitchen and living room."

Coop held up her phone to show me her schedule. "Then this is where I leave you in the capable hands of Higgs. I have three appointments this afternoon at Inkerbelle's and they're back to back. But he should be waiting outside for you now."

I winced. "You told him what we were doing here at the church?"

Coop tightened her scarf around her neck and nodded. "I texted him about why we were here and everything we learned from our anonymous man. I presume you're in for a tongue-lashing. It's too bad Higgs doesn't know how safe you really are with me, isn't it?" she asked, and I heard the subtext in her question.

Coop had been badgering me to tell Higgs about Artur, maybe even Knuckles and Goose, too. But I wasn't ready for that conversation yet. So I kept putting her off.

Shaking a warning finger at her, I narrowed my eyes. "I see what you're doing there, Coop."

"Do you, Trixie Lavender?" she asked in a haughty tone, one identical to the one Alexis Carrington used when she had a war of words with a foe.

I gave her a haughty look right back. "I do, and all in good time, my friend. All in good time."

As we stepped out into the gloomy day, I saw Higgs across the street and waved to him. He looked exhausted even from far away, and I couldn't blame him. The men at the shelter were like corralling greased cats on a good day.

With a killer on the loose? He was spitting in the wind, trying to keep them calm.

"Thanks for your help today, Coop. I don't know how I'd get through a single day without you."

She pulled the sides of her mouth up with her nimble fingers in the shape of a smile. "This is me, smiling at you."

I laughed as I skipped down the steps and prepared to talk Higgs into going to Sister Ophelia's with me. I really needed to get into her room and see if the TV Artur had drawn though me had something to do with her.

Higgs wasn't going to like it, especially if he knew what had just occurred in the confessional, and neither was Tansy, for that matter. So I wouldn't ask for permission. God helps those who help themselves, right?

Tsk-tsk, Trixie Lavender. You can't claim to disavow the Word and shed doubt on all you've been taught then turn around and use scripture for your own agenda. Shame on you.

That stab of guilt I felt when I relied on the Good Book's teachings after essentially shunning its message hit me square in the gut, but then I remembered. There was no shame in my game when it came to helping justice along its merry way. And I wanted justice for Sister Ophelia—no matter what it took.

"Sister Trixie Lavender," Higgs drawled, smiling down at me, his handsome face tanned and rugged, even in the gloom of the day. "What shenanigans are you knee-deep in today?"

I hooked my arm through his and giggled. "Funny you should ask…"

CHAPTER 11

*W*e'd decided to put going to Sister Ophelia's on hold after running into deacons Delacorte and Cameron on our way to her place.

Not that I suspected either of them. No. On the contrary. They were the last people on my list. But you never knew what someone might say that appeared meaningless to them, yet, turned out to be quite valuable to an investigation.

So we offered to buy them a cup of coffee at Betty's if they'd have a chat with us.

That happened just after Higgs gave me all sorts of flack for meeting a strange informant-like person in the church confessional. The deacons had no idea the stern talking to they'd saved me from.

As Delores served us in her funky, retro coffee shop, a place I'd come to love almost as much as I loved Inkerbelle's, I assessed the two men before me.

As we assembled in our chairs, Higgs and I on one side

of the table and the deacon's on the other, I smiled at them and their hesitant gazes.

Sometimes I still couldn't get over how handsome Deacon Delacorte was. His skin was the thing every female's dreams were made of. His olive complexion glowed with good health, his cheeks benefitted from a fresh patch of color on either side, and his eyelashes, so dark and thick, made me decide I needed to invest in better mascara. That he'd escaped marriage was either pure genius or by design.

On the other hand, Deacon Cameron looked positively harried. His eyes were red from what I figured was lack of sleep and steeped in concern as he looked at me. His pudgy hands curled around the brightly colored mug of black coffee.

"So how can we help you, Trixie? I think we told the police everything we knew already. Did we miss something?" Deacon Cameron asked.

I shook my head and sipped my own low-fat latté. "I don't know if you did or not. I just want to get a feel for what your relationship with Sister Ophelia was like. I know she liked you both. She said so just before she…died. But I have to wonder if you saw or heard anything you might not consider important, but in the scheme of things is vital to finding her killer."

Deacon Delacorte heaved a long sigh, his gorgeous eyes sad. He'd opted for a fresh cold glass of milk, endearing him even more to me.

"I can't tell you how much of an impression Sister Ophelia left on me. I had only a little interaction with her because, as you know, I'm new to Our Lady, but I enjoyed every moment because she was funny and warm and, most of all, welcoming. Though, as I said at the church the night this happened, and to the police when I gave my statement, we only talked about some scripture for the youth group's meeting, and we planned to meet later in the week once I'd researched some passages for her. Other than that, I didn't spend much time with her. To my deep regret," he said with a shadow of a smile.

"So you never saw her interact with anyone you didn't recognize or anyone suspicious?" Higgs asked, cupping his chin in his hand.

Deacon Delacorte firmly shook his head. "I didn't. Also, I've been busy settling into my new apartment and learning my duties at the church. It's been quite hectic."

"What made you go outside that night, Deacon Delacorte?"

"Please, call me Davis," he suggested, and then he sighed, lifting his broad shoulders. "I just needed a bit of fresh air."

Deacon Cameron nudged him with his elbow. "C'mon now. Tell them the truth, Davis. It'll get around anyway."

Both Higgs and I gave each other that look that said maybe we had something here, but Davis diffused that quickly.

He gave us a guilty glance, folding his lean hands in front of him. "Carla Ratagucci made me feel a little uncomfortable. Not a big deal in the grand scheme of things. I only wanted to escape for a moment."

"Hah! No big deal? Carla's a minx, always looking for her mate. She was a little inappropriate with Davis, is what he's trying to say. She made the moves on him the way she does every man within a hundred yards of her. He went outside to get away from her. That's the truth, and he shouldn't be shy about it."

But Davis's eyes were pleading—chocolate and melty and pleading. "Please understand, Miss Lavender. I don't want gossip to take center stage here. I don't want Miss Ratagucci harmed by any of this. You, as an ex-nun, must know what the church can be like when it comes to something of this nature. Please respect her privacy and keep this to yourself. She's had enough to deal with after finding that...after finding that body last night. She doesn't need more stress. I made it clear I wasn't interested and I escaped outside. That's all there was to it. I promise."

"Call me Trixie, please, and I promise the incident won't leave my circle of trust. But I *am* going to talk to Carla and confirm that. I don't have a choice. I hope you understand."

He sighed forlornly and looked into his mug of milk. "Of course. I understand, Trixie. You're just checking all the boxes."

I reached out and patted his hand for making such a gallant gesture in light of Carla's misbehavior. Not that it came as a surprise. He was right up Carla's alley. Single. Handsome. Breathing.

"She should know better, Trixie," Deacon Cameron protested. "Davis has been ordained for a very long time. He can't marry at this late stage in his career."

Well, there was that, too. "So you obviously didn't see anything other than Sister Ophelia's body on the ground, correct?"

"Honestly, I was so stunned by finding her, I couldn't believe it. My first instinct wasn't to look for anything suspicious. My first instinct was to look for her pulse. I thought she'd had a heart attack. But that wasn't the case." He let his chin fall to his chest then, and Deacon Cameron patted his arm in comfort. "I wish I had more to offer. I don't know how long she was out there, and I really don't know who would do something like this, but I can't get the image of her out of my head…"

Yeah. I knew the feeling. I decided to turn to Deacon Cameron, who'd known Sister Ophelia much better and far longer.

"Deacon Cameron? I guess the questions for you are the same. Did Sister Ophelia confide in you at all about anything she was upset about?"

Deacon Cameron blew out a breath, his acne-scarred cheeks inflating and releasing. "No. *Never*. We always had so many lovely conversations about our faith and lives, but she never confided any fear of anyone or anything. She was quite the joker, too, as I'm sure you know. We laughed often," he said, his tone suddenly somber and quiet. "I miss her laughter. I miss it a great deal."

I reached out and patted the back of his hand. "Me, too, Deacon Cameron. Me, too." On a sigh, I decided to wrap this up. "And lastly, do either of you have any idea who that was in the closet or how they could have gotten there?"

The image of that body flashed in my mind's eye, much as I'm sure it did the deacons', because they both turned pale and squirmed in their seats. Yet they both shook their heads in negative fashion, making me almost sigh out loud.

This was the Sahara Desert of questioning. It was dry. There wasn't anything here. Not that I could tell, anyway. Both Higgs and I knew it as we passed each other glances that said as much.

Taking the last sip of my coffee, I pulled a few dollars out of my purse, but Deacon Delacorte held up his hand as he, too, rose. "I've got this, Trixie," he offered generously as he pulled out an odd-looking piece of paper from his pocket, but he stopped short and gave me a sheepish grin. "Sorry. That's Chinese money. Must have left it in my pocket when I got back and forgotten about it. But no worries. Allow me, please."

"Thanks, Deacon Delacorte. Appreciate it."

I smiled at the deacons and stuck out my hand to Davis first—because, he looked so sad.

"Gentleman, thank you for entertaining my flights of fancy. You never know what could strike one person as totally inconsequential, only to find it's a very important detail. I just had to be sure nothing was missed. Thanks for indulging me. I hope to see you both at Sunday mass."

They both took my hand, but when I took Deacon Cameron's, he winced...and I noticed a small, round, bright red mark on the side of his broad hand.

He pulled his hand from mine and winced. "Lighting those candles in the rectory gets me every time," he complained with a brief smile before he followed Davis out of the dining area and headed to the door.

As Higgs and I made our exit, too, and we stepped out into the cool rain, I tucked my purse under my arm and asked, "Tell me something, Higgs."

He put his hand at my lower back, a gesture I'd come to welcome. "What would you like me to tell you, Sister Trixie?"

I stopped just as we made our way over the rough

terrain of the sidewalk, crossing my arms over my chest. "Did you see the mark on Deacon Cameron's hand?"

"I didn't see it closely, no."

"Couldn't that mark on his hand have been a burn mark from a cigarette? It's the right size and shape."

"What are you implying?"

"I'm implying that maybe we just let our killer get away. If he strangled Sister Ophelia while she still had a cigarette in her hand, when she reached up to pull his hands away from her neck, maybe she burned him?"

I demonstrated by wrapping my hands around my neck and pointing to the spot on my hand where Deacon Cameron's burn would land.

Higgs planted his hands on his hips and gave me a puzzled look. "Well, first, she'd have had to keep a pretty good grip on it. If he were strangling her, I imagine in her shock, she would have dropped it. Or maybe she used it as a weapon of sorts? To make the killer let her go. Either way, I guess it's entirely possible. But what's his motive, Trixie? According to him, and everyone around him, they had a good relationship. What's in it for him? What does he gain by murdering her? And why the brutality to it? Strangulation is an angry act. Deacon Cameron doesn't seem at all angry to me. He seems sad she's gone."

"Well, some people hide it better than others, don't they? We all hide our feelings from the world from time to time. Maybe Sister Ophelia made him angry."

"When you strangle someone to death, that's pretty angry, Trixie. Yes, the mark on his hand is suspicious because of Sister Ophelia's smoking, but I have trouble believing Deacon Cameron had anything to do with it. Either deacons, in fact."

"Maybe the cigarette was still in her mouth and when he went to strangle her, she nicked him with it?"

"Maybe," he replied, but he didn't sound at all convinced.

I flapped a hand at him and smiled as we began to walk again. "Fine. I'm just spit-balling here, but you're probably right. I mean, Deacon Cameron's a pussycat and Deacon Delacorte's too dreamy to strangle anyone."

Higgs's raven eyebrow rose in surprised fashion. "*Dreamy?*"

I grinned up at him. "Super-dreamy. Everyone says so."

"Oh, do they?" he drawled. "Define 'everyone.'"

"Careful, ex-Undercover Officer Higglesworth, your jealousy is showing."

"I'm not jealous. I'm just surprised. He's a man of the cloth. Carla, I understand. She's a bit forward about any man who interests her, but everyone thinks Deacon Delacorte's dreamy? *Everyone?*"

"He is indeed a man of the cloth, but a deacon can be attractive, Higgs. Carla's out of line, no doubt. But she treats most men that way."

Higgs made a mock swipe of his forehead. "Then I worry for Carla's immortal soul. You know, I was raised Catholic, but I don't remember any of the rules for deacons."

I popped my lips. "Some married men can become permanent deacons, but they need the consent of their wives and they have to marry before ordination. Deacon Dreamy is a transitional deacon, meaning he can't marry after his ordination and definitely can't marry after he's been ordained."

"As if it wasn't already confusing enough. I guess my lack of knowledge about the Catholic Church is showing."

Folding my hands behind my back, I asked, "You know, I've been meaning to ask you, how do you know Father Rico, anyway? I was surprised you knew a priest."

"I feel like you're insulting me, Trixie Lavender. Why is it so hard to believe I know a priest?"

Rolling my eyes, I giggled. "I don't mean it like that and you know it. I mean, I didn't know you were religious, per se."

"I guess I'm not really. Not in the technical sense anyway. I don't light candles or confess my sins or anything. I definitely don't have time to attend services, but I was raised Catholic and went to church with my family all the time. However, I do believe in being a good person, and if, in the end, Heaven exists and it's where I end up because I really tried to be a good person, great. If not, I just hope I end up in a place with burgers and steak."

I tipped my head back and laughed. "You know what they say about wish in one hand… You'd better be careful what you say out loud, or you're going to land in Soup or Salad for all eternity."

"Perish the thought," he joked with a grin. "Anyway, Father Rico. Um, we met at a racquetball court shortly after I moved here. His partner stood him up and so did mine, so we played against each other, hit it off, and we've been friendly ever since. He's a great resource for the shelter."

"Good to know. Did he ever tell you what the inspiration was for him to become a man of the cloth?"

Higgs put his hand at my elbow, guiding me around a

crowd of people outside a small luncheonette. "He didn't. How do *you* know what inspired him?"

I winked. "Tansy." As I told him what I'd learned about Father Rico's past, we continued walking until we were well into a pleasant-enough neighborhood lined with houses of similar height and shape.

We came to a stop in front of the modest building Sister Ophelia had lived in with some nuns from another order. I'd learned most of the nuns housed here were from St. Andrews, another Catholic church in Cobbler Cove, not Our Lady. So fortunately, no one would likely know me, which would work in my favor if my plans to get inside panned out.

The building was two stories in a deep red brick, with a nice walkway to the stairs lined with budding tulips and daffodils. The front porch was small but obviously put to good use, considering the rocking chairs and the little table between them with some kind of plant or another.

I hitched my thumb over my shoulder. "So, are you game to go fish around inside Sister Ophelia's?"

"How are you going to get inside, Trixie? Don't the nuns know you?"

"Nope. It's my understanding; most of the nuns here are from St. Andrews. They were kind enough to allow Sister Ophelia to move here recently because it's closer to Our Lady and the walking from her last residence was starting to bother her arthritic knees." I looked up at him and smiled. "So I ask again, are you up for a fishing expedition?"

Higgs gave me a skeptical glance, his eyes narrowing, his eyebrow rising. "Did Tansy give us permission to go fishing?"

"Nope again. She didn't answer me back when I asked, but the police have already done a search, and we *are* sort of already here..."

Higgs gave me that look he's so good at giving me when he disapproves of my tactics but wants in on the hunt.

I squinted up at him, standing against the backdrop of the gray clouds and sprouting trees, and asked, "Does that look mean I'm going it alone?"

He sighed, his broad chest inflating. "How exactly do you plan to get in there, Trixie? Wouldn't it just be easier to wait for Tansy's permission?"

I think we both knew Tansy wasn't likely to give me permission to do a search of Sister Ophelia's room. Sure, she gave me access to the people involved in a crime, but that was only after she'd had a right and proper go at them.

I got the leftovers, and that was fine—mostly. Sifting through someone's things was likely a whole different ball of wax—it was new territory I hadn't tested with her yet.

Plus, I really needed to see if what I'd sketched might have something to do with Sister Ophelia. Maybe she had a television that looked like the one I'd drawn—or rather the one Artur had drawn—which would, in all honesty, likely freak me out a little.

How was my demon seeing a personal item if it *did* turn out the TV was in Sister Ophelia's room, after all? I'd never been to Sister O's. I didn't even know where she'd lived until I'd asked another nun. Was Artur the Demon leaving my body and somehow running wild and free?

It's not as though I even knew he was there when he wasn't actively turning me into a raging bull. Maybe he had more power than even I knew and that made me shiver.

"Trixie?" Higgs said, cutting my scary thoughts off. "How do you plan to get into Sister O's room?"

I smiled at him. In fact, I summoned the best smile I knew how to smile. I summoned the fun, flirty smile Coop tried to replicate à la Joan Collins on *Dynasty*.

"How do I plan to get in there?" I drawled, widening my eyes before letting them smolder. "You're so silly. These were once my people, Oh, Ye of Little Faith. I'll do what I do best. Play the part of a grieving niece who happens to be an ex-nun."

CHAPTER 12

J knocked on the colorful door to the housing unit, praying whoever was in there would allow me inside.

When the periwinkle-blue door opened, a smiling, fresh face looked back at me. She had a sprinkling of freckles over the bridge of her nose, an innocent twinkle in her lovely dark brown eyes, and a beaming smile on her lips. She wore her full nun garb and a rosary at her hips that she busily threaded through her fingers.

And she looked like she was a brand-new nun, she was so bright-eyed and bushy-tailed. I hoped whoever was in charge up there would forgive me for what I was about to do to her. But I promise, I'm doing it for the greater good.

I couldn't tell anyone about the picture I drew, but I needed to see how or even *if* it related to Sister O's death. I know that sounds like I'm making justifications to suit my agenda, but there really wasn't any other way unless Tansy was willing to share anything she found, or I told her I'm possessed by a demon.

I suppose that would go over like a lead balloon. That left me with deception. I appease my conscience by calling it acting, but really, it's just a big fat lie I'll feel guilty about later.

Anyway, this obviously new nun looked quite cheerful. Her cheerfulness extended to her tone of voice. "Hello! How can I help you?"

I put on my best sad face and held out my hand, forcing tears to my eyes—which wasn't hard when I thought about how much I'd miss Sister O and our kibitzing over our favorite shows.

"Oh, hello," I said quietly. "My name is Trixie Lavender, and this is Cross Higglesworth. You are?"

She poked her head out the door and scanned the front porch before saying, "I'm Sister Linda. Can I help you?"

Reaching for Higgs's arm, I latched on to it as if I'd fall over were it not for his support and whispered, "I hope so, Sister Linda. I'm here on behalf of my aunt Ophelia…Sister Ophelia, that is."

Immediately, her face fell and she reached out a hand to me. "Oh, yes, Miss Lavender. I'm so very sorry for your loss."

I gulped and yanked a tissue from my purse to dab at my eyes. "Thank you. I know the police have already been here, so I thought maybe the time was right for me to drop by and take a peek at Aunt Ophelia's things."

Now her fresh face went from sympathetic to hesitant as she curled her fingers around the handle of the door. "Sister Ophelia was your aunt, you said?"

I noted she was waffling and, do or die, I had to get into Sister O's room. So I began to cry in earnest. "She was," I sniffled. "My dearly departed mother's sister. I even followed in her footsteps and became a nun, but—but—I..." I stopped, trailing off as though it were too much to go on, then I buried my head in Higgs's shoulder to depict my deep sorrow and shame, but mostly to hide my lying eyes.

Higgs, being Higgs, patted me on the back, obviously realizing he had no choice but to play along. And boy, did he ever.

"Sister Linda, this is a trying time for Trixie. It brings up a lot of really difficult memories for her. Memories of her expulsion from the convent. It was really an ugly time for all concerned with all sorts of words and phrases from her lawyers I still can't quite fathom. Time served and fifty hours of community service are just a few. Anyway, she and her aunt had just reconnected not long ago after a period of deep estrangement over Trixie's poor behavior and the shame she brought to her family. So as you can see, her aunt's death came as quite a shock. They never had the chance to meet in person after they came to an under-standing and all was forgiven."

With my face still buried in his chest, I pinched his hard abdomen. I was going to kill him for that whopper of a story. Rather than take Higgs out, I lifted my head and looked Sister Linda in the eye, giving her my best Bambi gaze, complete with yet more unshed tears and a trembling lower lip.

"My beloved boyfriend is right. We'd come so far in mending fences, and now, all I want to do is feel like I'm near her. I'll always regret not coming to visit sooner. And I find the thought of being surrounded by her things comforting. Just for a little bit. Please? Maybe I'll finally be able to sleep tonight. Do you mind? I promise I won't touch a thing." Dabbing at my eyes again, I let out a long, shuddering sigh.

But Sister Linda's face was white as a ghost as she looked from Higgs's face to mine. *"Your boyfriend?"*

I gave her a sheepish glance and winced as I took a step past her and into the threshold of the house. "Yes. I suppose you can see why my aunt was so upset with me now, and why I was stripped of my habit. Add in *his* sordid past and, well... But what can I say? Love is a powerful emotion. Besides, you do know what the Lord says about forgiveness, don't you? *Forgive as the Lord forgave you.* Surely that means Higgs should be forgiven for his gambling addictions and be worthy of love, doesn't it?"

I had to fight not to jump when Higgs pinched my waist.

Sister Linda's eyes were wide now when she mumbled, "Yes. That's what Colossians 3:13 says..."

I smiled sadly and sighed again. "Exactly. And my aunt came to see that Higgs isn't such a bad guy after all. He atoned for his casino debt, not to mention gave up the horse races and every last one of his loan-sharking clients. He's living a squeaky-clean life now, aren't you, light of my world?"

Only I noticed the narrowing of Higgs's eyes, but he nodded his head vigorously. "Indeed I am, sugarplum. Where would I be without your holy guidance?"

Now I grabbed on to Sister Linda's arm and took her with me toward the long stretch of hallway until we reached the bottom of a set of stairs, which I assumed would lead to the nuns' rooms.

"How well did you know my aunt, Sister Linda?"

She shrugged her shoulders but her smile was fond. "I loved Sister Ophelia, but I'm new, so I didn't know here terribly well."

"Did she ever mention anyone was upset with her?" I squeaked the words out, making it sound as though the mere thought was torture. "Upset enough to *kill* her?"

Sister Linda's face fell. "Oh, no! I found her quite delightful, and as I told the police yesterday, everyone here loved her. I'd never seen anything suspect."

I let my chin drop to my chest for a moment before I lifted my eyes to meet hers. "That's what the police said, too." Letting out yet another long, woebegone sigh, I said, "So if you'll just tell me where my aunt's room was, I'll sneak up there quick like a bunny and be well out of your hair in plenty of time for vespers." I pointed up the burgundy carpeted steps and looked at her hopefully.

"Of course. Third room on the right," she murmured before she escaped to another room in the back of the house.

I beat feet up the stairs to avoid the possibility she'd change her mind and headed to Sister O's room down along a stark hallway with nothing but a picture of Jesus on the wall. Pulling on some sterile gloves, I handed a pair to Higgs before popping the door open.

Once we were inside, I closed the door and leaned back against it, narrowing my eyes at Higgs. *"The shame I brought to my family?"* I hissed at him, giving him the evil eye.

He shot me a cocky smile. "Um, at least that's better than a gambling addiction and my job as a loan shark."

On tippy-toe, I jabbed a finger under his nose. "Are you

taking a class in creative writing, or what? I could kill you for that whopper."

He chuckled. "But you won't, because then you wouldn't have me to help you make up outlandish stories to get you into places you shouldn't be in the first place."

"Touché, Tom Clancy."

He grinned as he looked around Sister O's very stark room. "It's pretty bare in here, huh?"

"Well, they don't have a lot of Earthly possessions. That's just the way of being a nun. But Sister Ophelia really *didn't* have much at all, did she?"

As I scanned the small room, with a bathroom and shower attached to it, I didn't see a TV. So whatever Artur had seen—if he'd seen anything and he wasn't just playing with me—it wasn't here in Sister O's room.

There were very few personal items. A black and white picture on her nightstand of what I assumed was Sister O as a baby and her parents. Both attractive people, dressed in smart clothes and fancy hats outside a church, held a chubby Sister Ophelia in their arms. If the fashion said anything, it screamed sometime in the 1940s, which made it around the right time Sister O would have been born.

There was a worn, blue and beige, hand-knitted blanket on the edge of her white cast iron bed, a pillow and some blankets. A rosary hung from a mirror over her chipped yellow oak dresser, along with a mass card of the Lord's Prayer tucked into the mirror. A well-loved Bible sat atop the scarred surface, along with some ornamental glass bottles in dark blue and green.

Her bathroom held nothing more than some soap, shampoo, conditioner and deodorant, and a lone bottle of hand lotion. I pulled open the drawers of her vanity to find some heat-related creams for muscle cramps, aspirin, some acid relief, towels and washcloths.

And that was pretty much that.

Standing up straight, I planted my hands on my hips. Sister O had always talked about watching reruns of *Unsolved Mysteries* and *CSI*, but there was no evidence of a TV or anything in her room. There wasn't even a radio.

Maybe she watched in a common area somewhere else in the house?

Higgs poked his dark head around the corner of the bathroom and wrinkled his nose. "I didn't find anything in the dresser drawers or the closet. Just some extra habits, shoes, and nun stuff. Did you find anything in here?"

"Nope. So all that playing pretend and we still got nothing."

"Maybe Tansy found something."

I made a face at his hopeful reflection in the mirror. "If she did, it's something she's not telling me about, that's for sure." Sighing, I decided it was time to move on. I still had Sister Patricia and Carla to talk to. "I guess we'd better go, huh? I need to check in on the gang at the shop anyway, and then there's Sister Patricia, of course."

"I don't envy you that conversation."

I blew out a breath of air. "Me neither. But it has to be done."

As he opened the door, he whispered, "You don't really think she's capable of murder, do you? She's kind of crabby, but murder?"

I looked up into his handsome face. "Well, she is committing the sin of all sins, Higgs. With a parent of a student, no less. It's certainly an infraction worthy of murder, and it's not like Sister Patricia and Sister O were friends. There was no love lost between them to begin with. With the threat of Sister O giving her up to Father Rico in the mix? It could have been enough to push her over the edge."

He clucked his tongue at me and opened the door wide. "I don't know. I'm not sure I'm buyin' what you're sellin' this time. I think I need more proof mean old Sister Patricia's capable of murder. Either way, let's get out of here, my wayward nun." He hitched his jaw toward the hallway.

"Why the hurry? You have some legs you need to break, loan shark?" I asked in my best New York accent.

We both laughed as we made our way back down the austere staircase to find Sister Linda at the bottom, her young, open face with a smile still plastered on it.

"How are you feeling, Miss Lavender?"

I breathed out a long, belabored sigh and let my shoulders droop. "A little better, thank you. It was wonderful to see Aunt Ophelia's things. I know she didn't have much, but just being where she once rested her head was a great comfort."

She held out her hand to me and smiled sweetly. "I'm so glad I could aid in helping you find some peace."

"You're a godsend." Then I paused thoughtfully. "You know, Sister Linda, Aunt O mentioned she watched a lot of one show or another." I snapped my fingers and pretended to think, then shook my head as though I couldn't come up with the title. "Gosh, I can't remember the name of it now, but she said she watched it all the time. Yet, I didn't see a television in her room."

Sister Linda nodded her head knowingly. "Ah, yes. She loved reruns of *Unsolved Mysteries* on Amazon Prime."

Wow. The church had gone kicking and screaming into the new millennium, eh? "You have Internet here?"

She chuckled and patted my arm. "I know most people don't think we're hip to the times, but we have all the amenities, including VCRs."

I gave her a blank stare, but she flapped her hands at me and laughed again. "I'm teasing. But seriously, we have running water, cable, and even a Google Home device."

I chuckled at her joke and peeked over her shoulder at the living room. There was a television, for sure, but it looked nothing like the one Artur had drawn. "Oh dear. I'm sorry. Anyway, did she watch it on the TV there?" I pointed over her rounded shoulder.

"Oh, no. She liked her peace and quiet when she came in from spending the day with the children. She watched in her room on her iPad. In fact, just before she was murd— Er, went to meet our Heavenly Father, Sister Rita told her if she didn't get a set of earplugs, she was going to throw Sister Ophelia's iPad out the window. Of course, she didn't mean it, but it was quite loud. Sister Rita's room is right next door to Sister Ophelia's."

I wondered about this Sister Rita. Could she be a suspect? People had killed for far less…

I nodded my head as though I knew Sister O was hard of hearing. "She was a little hard of hearing, so I can understand Sister Rita's frustration. But what happened to her iPad?"

Now Sister Linda frowned, cupping her hand over her throat. "You know, I don't know. I don't recall the police taking it. There wasn't much to take to begin with. Oh, heavens. I'm sorry. I'll make sure someone looks for it."

"No-no. I'm sure it'll turn up. Don't you worry yourself over it, but…is there any chance Sister Rita might know where it is?"

She blinked at us. "I don't know, but I could ask her if you'd like. If you'll leave your number, I'd be happy to give you a call."

Higgs gave me that confused look over Sister Linda's head, but I poo-pooed her and smiled wider. "Bah! No worries. I can always drop back by and ask her myself. Maybe I'll get a chance to spend a little time with my aunt's things again. Anyway, we really have to run. Higgs has a GA meeting to get to—"

"And Trixie has her two hours of community service for her little," he lowered his voice and gave Sister Linda a conspiratorial wink of his eye, "brush with the law."

Oh, I was going to kill him so hard when we got out of here!

For now, I had to give him one of my cute smiles and nod in agreement. "My honeybuns is right. We really have to get going, but I hope you know your kindness has meant the world to me. Thanks again."

Sister Linda walked us to the door and waved us off. I'm pretty sure I heard a sigh of relief gush from her throat, but we didn't look back.

As we hit the sidewalk, I didn't have time to give Higgs a piece of my mind because I got a text from Tansy. Scanning it, a cold chill ran up my spine, making my hand tighten around my phone.

"Hey! Wayward nun, what's going on?"

"It's… It's Sister Patricia," I managed to say.

"Is she our next hit?"

"No…" I murmured in confusion. "I think she'll be too busy in interrogation. She's been arrested for the murder of Sister Ophelia."

CHAPTER 13

*A*s I sat in a church pew with Father Rico and deacons Delacorte and Cameron, hoping to console them about Sister Patricia's arrest, I still didn't understand what had happened, and Tansy was officially unavailable to consult—which meant she was likely in the middle of questioning Sister Patricia.

I hadn't even heard back on the hasty text I'd sent about my mystery-man meeting or whether the school had cameras positioned by the coat closet so said mystery man could be identified. But my lost-his-faith-in-humanity mystery man was the least of my concerns at this point.

Father Rico needed our attention most right now. I patted his hand as Higgs handed him a freshly brewed cup of tea and Deacon Cameron wrapped a sweater around his wide shoulders.

He gave Higgs and the deacons a wan smile. "Thank you, Cross, Trixie, and you both, as well. You're all such a blessing."

I felt horrible for him and wondered if this crime

reminded him of his own brush with a criminal all those years ago. I decided that conversation was for another time and place. Right now we had bigger fish to fry. If this was dredging up old memories for Father Rico, I hoped he knew he could talk to me.

Turning in my seat, I looked at him. "Father Rico, what did Detective Primrose say again? On what grounds did they arrest Sister Patricia?"

He sighed, cupping the mug of tea Higgs had brought him. "Detective Primrose said she was arresting her on suspicion of murder. That was *all* she said. Then she read her those Mira rights, cuffed her and put her in a car to take her to the station."

His misery was clear as a bell. His lined face screamed tortured. "Oh, Father Rico. I'm so sorry."

"It was awful, Trixie. Sister Patricia was beside herself. She sobbed the entire way out of the church. Watching her taken away like that... I don't think I can believe she's capable of murder. I just can't," he moaned.

I wasn't going to be the one to tell him Sister Patricia probably wouldn't be coming back to the church whether she was innocent or not. Not once he found out about her breaking her vows.

"I'm so sorry, Father Rico," I murmured with a clenching heart.

He shook his rapidly graying head. "I shouldn't have brushed Sister Ophelia off that night in favor of my duties as host. Surely, whatever she wanted to tell me had to do with her death. My entire church is crumbling right before my very eyes, and I can't seem to do a thing about it!"

"Now, that's not true, Father," Deacon Delacorte

soothed, his beautiful face forcing a smile I know he didn't truly feel. "We'll figure this out. We'll pool together our resources and find a good lawyer for Sister Patricia. Surely we can appeal to the diocese or someone in the chain of command."

Deacon Cameron cleared his throat and patted Father Rico on the back. "Davis is right, Father. We'll put our heads together and figure this out. Don't worry about that for now. Just catch your breath."

Sighing, I patted his beefy hand once more. "It's been a rough couple of days for Our Lady, for sure. I'm sorry this has fallen on your shoulders."

Higgs waggled a finger at me and pointed to the vestibule. I excused myself for a moment and treaded out to see what was going on.

He held up his phone, pointing to the screen. "Tansy just called me. First, more prelim findings from the coroner. Sister Ophelia's larynx was crushed. They're releasing that information to the public later today."

All the color drained from my face. How absolutely awful.

"She just finished questioning Sister Patricia."

My stomach dropped to my feet and my heart began that erratic rhythm I've become so familiar with. "And?"

He grated a sigh. "And naturally, Sister Patricia swears she didn't kill Sister O, but I heard Tansy say they have a witness who claims they heard Sister Patricia confessed to killing her. She thought she'd put me on hold, but she really had me on *speakerphone.* I guess one of the officers was in the process of reporting back to her. Lucky for us, I heard most of what was said."

If Jesus himself walked into the church right that very second and told me the meaning of life, I couldn't have been more floored.

"Sister Patricia *confessed?*" I squeaked, my eyes bulging out of my head. "To the police?"

"No. The witness claims she heard Sister Patricia confess to the person she was talking to on the phone."

My jaw almost unhinged. "Who's the witness?"

"*Mrs. Coletti*—whose first name is Mira, by the way—is the witness...and *Horatio Coletti* was who was on the other end of that phone call. Apparently, Sister Patricia and *Horatio* were having an affair."

A vision of the fancy Mrs. Coletti, with her jewelry, furs, and perfect hair, alongside her short, overcompensating husband, flashed through my brain.

Still, I blinked in shock. I wasn't past the part of this tale that included a confession from Sister Patricia let alone an affair.

I held up a hand, my brow furrowed. "Okay, wait. Daniel's mother claims she heard Sister Patricia confess to Horatio Coletti that she killed Sister O? I... I don't understand. On what planet would Sister Patricia take a phone call anywhere in the vicinity of Mira Coletti?"

"Mira claims she heard *Horatio* on the phone, talking with Sister Patricia. She'd suspected him of an affair for a while, so she began to lurk behind the scenes during his phone conversations. I guess she didn't ever suspect the affair she'd catch him having would be with a nun."

If I'd had trouble understanding a motive to murder Sister O before, I was *really* having trouble digesting the fact that the man Sister Patricia was having an affair with was

Horatio Coletti. I didn't want to cast judgment, but she was certainly the exact opposite of Mrs. Coletti. Though, maybe that's why Mr. Coletti was drawn to her in the first place.

"*Sister Patricia…*" I murmured again, still in shock.

Higgs nodded his head. "Yep. And apparently, Sister Patricia confirmed she was indeed having an affair with Daniel's father."

Oh, mercy.

I reached out and gripped his forearm. "Okay, so let me get this straight. Mira Coletti actually heard her husband talking to Sister Patricia about a plot to kill Sister Ophelia?"

I realize I was repeating myself, but dang. I couldn't have been more shocked.

"That's what she says. She claims she found out after overhearing a phone conversation between the two of them, and she confronted Mr. Coletti."

"So they kill Sister O because they're afraid she's going to tell Father Rico about breaking her vows? Why would Mr. Coletti care what Sister O did with the information?"

"Well, Mira claims Sister Patricia and her husband were in cahoots together because they both couldn't afford to get caught playing around. Mr. Coletti due to a pretty ironclad prenup, and Sister Patricia for obvious reasons."

I frowned, hard, rubbing my temple with two fingers. "But wait, doesn't that just sound like revenge to you, Higgs? Mrs. Coletti's angry with her husband for having an affair—and believe me, I'm still blown away the affair was with Sister Patricia—she's so angry, she decides to create a story about Sister Patricia confessing to murdering Sister O. The end result being, Mr. Coletti loses his lover *and* his money, *and* he and his lover get the ultimate punishment."

"Well, phone records indicate they've been in constant contact with one another before and after the murder."

"Well, sure they are. They're having an affair!" I said in exasperation.

Higgs held up a hand and frowned. "But that's not the worst of it."

I gripped the strap of my purse and braced myself. "Oh, dear. Go ahead. Hit me."

"Carla Ratagucci confirmed that Sister Patricia went outside the exit door after Sister Ophelia the night of the murder. Her claim is, she never mentioned it because never in a million years did she think Sister Patricia would be the guilty party. Then she was so shook up by the headless corpse, she forgot until today."

"She forgot…" How did you forget something as important as that?

"That's what she said. She also claims she doesn't know the amount of time between when Sister Patricia went outside to speak to Sister Ophelia, and when Davis dragged her body inside. Carla claims she was too distracted by the activities of the speed dating to remember."

I reached out and put my palm on the wall to steady myself. "So, Carla's story gives validity to the theory that Sister Patricia killed Sister O. Are we buying that story? Maybe Carla's angry with Sister Patricia about something we don't know about, and she wants revenge?"

I knew that sounded like a stretch, but I was open to anything at this point.

Higgs ran a hand through his thick hair and stretched his neck. "I don't know, Trixie, but according to the officer who relayed this information to Tansy, Mrs. Coletti's pretty staunch about her claim that she heard Mr. Coletti on the phone in collusion with Sister Patricia."

"Boy," I marveled at our good fortune and something as simple as speaker phone. "That was some phone call, huh?"

Higgs grinned and winked. "Tansy stinks at technology. She's always struggled with computers and cell phones. But listen, in all fairness, we have to keep all of these details under wraps, Trixie. I wasn't supposed to hear any of that, and you know as well as I do, Tansy would put us in a cell before she'd risk a leak like this in the investigation. The only official word is Sister Ophelia's larynx was crushed and the killer's still at large."

I held up my fingers in Scout's honor fashion. "I'll keep it between us—and maybe Coop. You don't have to worry about her. She's like Fort Knox."

Higgs crossed his arms over his chest. "So, theories?"

"Has anyone thought about the fact that Mrs. Coletti drinks? Or that Mrs. Coletti's likely feeling pretty spiteful after finding out her husband's having an affair with a *nun*? And how exactly do they suppose Sister Patricia, who weighs maybe a hundred pounds soaking wet, strangled Sister O with such brutality she had numerous bruises on her neck?"

Higgs held up his hands and shook his head. "I'm sure Tansy will ask those questions and more. She's also arrested Horatio, if that makes any of this better, but that's all I have for right now. Remember, I'm just the messenger and a lowdown dirty one at that."

Pulling my phone out, I muttered, "I need to speak to Sister Patricia. I need to hear this from the horse's mouth. This makes no sense, Higgs. Okay, so Sister Patricia was having a tawdry affair with a married man and she told Sister O about it, but to kill her over it in an effort to keep anyone from finding out about her behavior? I'm really struggling with that theory. If it were anyone else, it might be different, but this isn't working for me on a million levels. And lest we forget the headless corpse? I mean, is that connected or just some random murder? Is Sister Patricia some kind of crazed killer gone on a rampage? I really need to talk to her."

Higgs cast me a sympathetic look. "You do realize Tansy's not going to let you talk to Sister Patricia, don't you? They can hold her for forty-eight hours. So you'd have to wait, even if she *hasn't* already lawyered up, and no decent lawyer is going to let her talk to you, either."

Higgs was right, but I had to do something or I was going to crawl out of my skin. "Are you okay to stay with Father Rico and the deacons? I need some air."

He winked at me and squeezed my shoulder. "You bet. Call me if you think of anything else you want to talk over, okay? Maybe we'll meet tonight for dinner?"

I nodded my head and waved over my shoulder. I was too deep in my head to think about dinner or talking, or anything other than the fact that I didn't believe Sister Patricia had anything to do with this.

Did I believe Horatio Coletti had, and he was letting her take the fall for him? You bet. He was a shark who was used to getting his own way. And I didn't care that he was allegedly on a plane home from Vancouver when it happened. Anything was possible—including the idea that he'd talked Sister P into killing for him in the name of love.

Maybe.

I shook my head. I just couldn't swallow that story. I was going around in circles and that wasn't helping anything.

I really needed some space to clear the fog in my head this particular murder had become. All I kept coming up with was blank spots, and I needed to fill in those blanks.

I was going to go back over the facts in the peace and quiet of my office at the shop, but before I did, I wanted to take a peek at the alleyway where Sister O had met her fate.

I'm not sure why I needed to do that. I'd avoided it thus far, but today, I felt compelled to at least look at the crime scene.

I scooted around the side of the church in the pouring rain and stared down the alleyway leading to the exit door in the basement. As I made my way toward the spot where Sister Ophelia had been found, I remembered our laughter when I'd unwittingly caught her smoking, and tears sprang to my eyes.

I realize there was likely nothing there for me to see, but walking the path she'd walked before her death renewed my vow to find her real killer—not the one Mrs. Coletti would like us to *believe* was the killer.

Her motive to lie about what she'd heard between her husband and his lover wasn't exactly new. Revenge came in many forms, and jealousy was number one. But wow, that was bold, not to mention, hearsay.

The question was, did she have proof to back up her claim? And why hadn't Sister Patricia mentioned she'd talked to Sister Ophelia just before she was killed?

I looked up to the gray, ugly sky and closed my eyes. "I'm trying, Sister O. I really am. I know you didn't like Sister

Patricia, and she was committing an egregious sin, but I don't believe she killed you. I simply don't."

With those words, the rain began to come down in buckets, splashing my face and making me shake my finger up at the sky in warning.

Still, I chuckled. "Knock it off. You know what the Lord says about being petty. Sister Patricia didn't do it, and you know I'm right. Now either be helpful or butt out."

Ironically, the rain quite suddenly stopped.

I winked upward, heading toward the sidewalk and off to the shop with a fond grin on my face, and in my mind's eye, a vision of Sister Ophelia laughing down on me from a cottony white cloud.

CHAPTER 14

"*T*rixie girl?" Knuckles said from outside my office door. "Can I come in?"

I rubbed my eyes and yawned, pushing Coop's phone away. She'd let me have a look at it because it had pictures of the speed-dating event and Sister Ophelia's body. Unfortunately, the pictures had absolutely nothing to help me identify a killer.

So I could certainly use a break from the task of finding absolutely nothing.

"C'mon in, Knuckles. I'm not doing anything but going 'round in circles anyway."

And that was just the truth. I'd scoured the pictures Coop had taken of the people at the event with a fine-tooth comb and saw nothing suspicious.

She'd even taken a couple right near the exit door, but nothing with Sister Ophelia in them. Not before she was killed, anyway. There were, however, plenty pics of the female congregation fawning over Deacon Delacorte. In fact, Coop was quite the photographer. She'd used all sorts of fancy filters to brighten and lighten or even age some of the photos, and there were lots of them with female parishioners from Our Lady.

The one of the deacons, arm in arm, wide grins on their faces, was especially well done. Maybe I'd frame it and bring it to Father Rico as a way to cheer him up.

I'd also gone over the church's Facebook page for any sign of anything peculiar and come up dry. In fact, Father Rico, or whoever was in charge of the church's social media, didn't post with great frequency.

There was a welcome post from Father Rico to Deacon Delacorte, and plenty of well wishes from the congregation for his return from his mission in China, but certainly no suspicious comments. The announcement about Sister Ophelia's candlelight vigil was the most recent post, and Coop was right. Nothing suspicious there, either.

So what did I have? A bunch of suspects who had alibis except Sister Patricia. That's what I had. The trouble was, her motive to kill Sister O was the strongest of them all, aside from possibly Mr. Coletti.

"Hey, you okay, kiddo?" he asked, his concerned gaze perusing my face. Gosh, I loved Knuckles. He'd become like a father to me and Coop.

I smiled and pushed the papers I'd been making notes on into a messy pile. "I'm just doing what I do."

He nodded his head, the glint of his eyebrow piercings catching the lights overhead. "Murder board?"

"More like going-nowhere board. I'm stumped, Knuck, and now they have Sister Patricia in custody with a statement from Mrs. Coletti that's pretty damaging."

He winked at me and shot me a sympathetic smile. "You always say that, and then out of nowhere, you figure it out."

I snorted. "The trouble is, I figure it out when it's almost too late. You do remember the last crime I was involved in, right?"

Knuckles grinned at me. "I have every faith you're honing those skills with each case you solve, and in no time, you'll be able to open your own detective agency."

I hopped up from my chair and held my arms out. "Hug me, mister. You're good for my self-esteem."

He wrapped his burly arms around me and gave me a tight hug before he said, "Speaking of faith. There's a Sister Rita from Saint Andrews here to see you."

That made me stop cold. "Sister Rita from the house where Sister O lived?"

"I don't know and I didn't ask, kiddo. She's a nun. A cheerful enough looking one, mind you. But when I see a holy lady, I immediately turn into my fourth grade self. Which means I shut my trap and stay in line."

I swatted his arm playfully and wrinkled my nose. "You make us sound like the monsters of religion."

He dropped a kiss on the top of my head. "They didn't make 'em like you back in my day, young lady. You want me to send her in or will you come out?"

I gave him a quick kiss on his cheek. "I'll come out. Thanks, Knuckles."

He reached over me and grabbed the store tablet, the one we used to schedule appointments and set reminders for store events, and held it up. "I'm taking this with me for a minute. I'll bring it right back. I need to update my appointments for next week, okay?"

"Yep. Thanks for keeping on top of it. Goodness knows I'm doing a pretty poor job of much since this happened."

I followed him out into the lounge of the shop and waved a hand to Sister Rita, who sat on our puffy royal-blue couch surrounded by some graphic throw pillows of Marilyn Monroe and Mick Jagger, looking so completely out of place, I had to stop myself from chuckling.

She was a tiny little thing, cute as a button, in fact. Her eyes were quick, darting from corner to corner in the shop, with her hands neatly folded in her lap but one foot tapping to the music on the speaker system.

"Sister Rita?" Holding out my hand, I smiled warmly, hoping she didn't feel too uncomfortable in a tattoo shop.

She hopped up, spry as the day is long for someone her age, which I pegged at about sixty or so, and didn't outwardly appear at all disturbed by her surroundings. "Trixie Lavender, is it?"

"It is. Lovely to meet you. I'm so glad you dropped by, Sister Rita."

She grabbed my hand with her petite one and gave it a quick squeeze, bobbing her head. "Nice to meet you, too. I'm so sorry about your aunt, Trixie. We had some really terrific discussions. Late into the night some nights. I'll miss them so much. I only wish we'd had more time to get to know one another before..."

A bit of guilt began to settle in when she mentioned my "aunt." Before, back at the Sister O's house, I'd been caught up in the moment of improv, but faced directly with my bold lie, I felt immense shame as she smiled at me so cheerfully.

I fought hard to focus on her and not my guilt. "I'll miss her, too."

She brushed her hands down the front of her modest skirt and pulled the purse she had on her shoulder around to the front of her body, reached inside and pulled out an iPad. "Anyway, Sister Linda mentioned you'd been by, and you were wondering what happened to your aunt's iPad. Voila," she said with a gleam in her eye.

Stab. Stab. Stab. That was more guilt poking at me. But I pushed ahead because what choice did I have? "Oh, yes! I'd completely forgotten about that, but you didn't have to come all the way over here, Sister Rita. I'd have been happy to drop back to your place."

She looked down at her plain black lace-up shoes for a moment before her twinkling brown eyes met mine with guilt in them.

"I have a confession to make, Trixie. I stole this from Ophelia. In the mess of her death, I'd forgotten all about it. And I guess 'stole' isn't the right word. It was more like I hijacked it," she said with a small chuckle.

"Hijacked it?"

With a roll of her eyes, she nodded, holding the tablet out to me. "Oh, her hearing was dreadful, Trixie. Just dreadful! Our rooms were right next door to one another. She'd listen to that thing so loud when she watched her programs, I wanted to throw it out the window! In fact, I threatened to do just that the very night she…died. So when she left to go to the event at Our Lady, I snuck into her room and took it from her. I really *was* just going to take it to the computer store and find out what kind of ear thingamajigs it needed so she could use them, and I could get some sleep. But then... Well, you know what happened next. I darn well forgot all about it until Sister Linda mentioned you'd asked after it. I'm sorry, Trixie."

Now, of course, I should send her to the Cobbler Cove police with the iPad, but is it *my* fault she brought it to me first, and I forgot to mention she should bring it to the police?

My smile was of gratitude. "Oh, thank you, Sister Rita. I appreciate it, and no hard feelings. You were just trying to find a solution. Ophelia could be pretty stubborn."

She tucked her aging hands around her purse strap and peered at me. "Any news yet on who might have done this?"

I didn't have to fake the slump in my shoulders one bit. "No. Nothing yet." Pausing, I gave her a thoughtful glance. "Did you ever see anything suspicious? See *anyone* suspicious around your place? Did you see anything that might help us find out who did this?"

Reaching out, she wrapped her fingers around my wrist. "I wish I could help you, Trixie, but no. I never saw anyone who would lead me to believe they would commit something as horrible as murder. We're all so distraught over the very notion someone would harm a nun, of all people. Especially because it appears so random and with no motive. Ophelia was a wonderful member of the community, and her death has left us all reeling. I only wish I could help you more."

Me, too. "So she didn't seem upset over anything—maybe have a confrontation with someone that didn't come off as a big deal then, but might mean something now?"

Sister Rita gave a hard shake to her head. "No. Never. Ophelia was opinionated, but she certainly never inspired confrontation. She was always smiling and joking, and though I only knew her for a mere two weeks since she'd moved in, I genuinely liked her, if not the volume on her iPad."

Sighing, I offered my hand to Sister Rita again. "Then thank you again for dropping this to me, and for taking time out of your day to do it. I hope we'll have the chance to share a conversation sometime when things aren't so fraught."

"Happy to help, Trixie. Blessings to you and yours." She gave me a wink and a nod and she was off, slipping through the people entering the shop with lithe movements.

As I watched her stride down the sidewalk from the shop's picture window, I marveled at the pep in her step until she disappeared into the crowd.

Clinging to the iPad, I took it with me to my office and sat it on my desk, wanting to open it and look and see what I could find. But the idea it could be evidence held me back —mostly. Also something to factor in: surely it would be password protected, and I'm no hacker. I couldn't even imagine what a nun would use as a password anyway.

But that didn't keep me from desperately wanting to flip it open and pore over the contents. I had to set it on my desk next to the one Knuckles had returned and physically walk away to avoid temptation.

Just then, a group of customers came in, taking my mind off waiting for Tansy to text me with any morsel of information on Sister Patricia, and away from Sister Ophelia's dang iPad.

~

"*T*rixie?"

I looked up from my paperwork on my desk and cocked my head at Coop. "Hey, you. You ready to go home, maybe grab some dinner on the way? Higgs wanted to meet up. Naturally, he's talking a burger joint. Does Killer Burger appeal?"

She nodded and held up the store's tablet. "Yes. I love their peanut-butter-bacon-pickle burger. Yum-yum," she responded in her wooden tone. "I'm done for the day, but before we go, I thought you said we weren't allowed to use the tablet for anything but store business?"

With a frown, I pushed my chair from my desk and rose to stretch. "Well, I'd prefer we didn't, if only for tax purposes. I try to be honest with the taxman when I say I bought it to keep track of store appointments and events. Why do you ask?"

"When you were with those customers, I grabbed it from your desk to enter my appointments for the coming week and it wasn't charged. So I charged it, but when I opened it, *Unsolved Mysteries* was on pause."

My heart jumped in my chest as I put two and two together. "Oh, dear. You must have grabbed Sister Ophelia's iPad by mistake. They're identical. Sister Rita, a nun she lived with, dropped it by today."

Coop eyeballed me and lifted her chin. "Why would she bring you Sister O's iPad, Trixie?"

I winced in more shame, preparing for my Coop lecture. "Weeell, I did a little snooping earlier today." I explained what I'd done, and Coop clucked her tongue.

"*You lied, Trixie.*"

I gave her a guilty look. "But it was for the greater good."

"Does the greater good involve you making up an outrageous story about Higgs?"

Pursing my lips, I gave her a sheepish glance. "He made them up about me, too," I responded in a childish bid for neener-neener-neener.

"If he jumped off a bridge, would you do the same?"

Oh, dear. The grasshopper had become the sensei. "He'd never jump off a bridge. I think he's afraid of heights," I joked.

"Trixie…" she said, her admonishing tone, usually saved for when Livingston did something she thought was dishonest, in full warning mode.

"Okay, look, I'm just trying to figure out what happened to Sister O. And I didn't open it or even look at it. Plus, I texted Tansy to tell her I had it." I held up my phone to show her the text. "See?"

"All I'm hearing is excuses, Sister Trixie Lavender," she said over her shoulder as she left my office.

I stuck my tongue out at her. Behind her back, of course. I mean, she could break me in half if the mood is right. No reason to tempt the gods…but that left me alone with Sister Ophelia's enticing iPad.

The iPad on which she'd been doing what she loved doing best—watching a mystery. And let's not forget how convenient it was that her iPad wasn't password protected.

I call sign. Yes. That was exactly what this was. It was certainly a sign from somewhere, yes?

So I walked my fingers across the desk and touched the screen because I couldn't help myself, okay?

Sure enough, true to form, she had been watching

Unsolved Mysteries. Season twelve, episode ten on Amazon Prime. Maybe I'd watch that tonight in her honor while I stewed in my misery at my inability to solve the mystery surrounding her death.

Lingering on the screen, I thought long and hard about looking at any files she might have, or emails, but then I snatched my hand away, ashamed of myself.

Coop was right. There was the greater good and there was the greater need to snoop—of which I was surely guilty. Turning my back on my desk, I grabbed my purse, my dismal notes and my jacket, and left my office to head out and meet Higgs.

But I took the iPad with me.

It was, after all, police evidence, right?

We couldn't just leave something that could turn out to be important just lying around, could we?

CHAPTER 15

"So, where are we?" Higgs asked as he stuffed a crispy fry in his mouth as we finished up our dinner.

I wiped my lips with my napkin and scoffed. "Absolutely the same stinkin' place we were when I left you at the church earlier. Nowheresville. Unless we want to consider Deacon Cameron. He did have a burn on the side of his hand."

"He did," Higgs agreed. "But what else do we have on him other than that? Maybe you should look at some of the timestamps on the pictures you told me Coop took and see where he was when Sister Ophelia was killed."

There was that. "I already did, and it doesn't look like he ever left the basement of the church, but that doesn't mean he couldn't have and it doesn't mean Deacon Delacorte wouldn't have either."

"Nope. It doesn't. So we'll put them in our longshot pile because we don't have a choice."

I sighed. Higgs was right, and I was getting antsy. "Any news from Tansy?"

He peeked at his phone on the table. "Nope. Nothing."

Chewing on a pickle, I mused, "You know, I've been thinking all day about the headless corpse and Sister Patricia. *If*—and I use that loosely—if Sister Patricia really did kill Sister O, you can't possibly think she killed the headless guy, too, can you? I mean, if you think strangulation is brutal, what is chopping up a body?"

"What is insane, Alex?" Higgs said, his answer spoofing *Jeopardy*.

"Exactly. I don't believe she's capable of that kind of torture."

"You'd be surprised what people are capable of, Trixie." Higgs said, giving me his ex-undercover cop warning tone.

I held up my index finger. "Okay, you're right, but let's say you're not. If she really killed Sister O, how is the guy in the closet related to Sister Ophelia? And if she didn't kill Sister Ophelia or anyone, who killed the guy in the closet? And why? Does that mean there are two killers? Or do they have the wrong one? Either way, a killer's still on the loose."

Higgs's head dipped low as he looked at his plate. "Tell me about it. The guys at the shelter are a wreck."

Fear sizzled along my spine. "Please tell me Solomon is tucked in for the night?"

Higgs winked and nodded his head. "He is. He's been on time for bed check ever since Dr. Mickey's murder."

Rubbing my temples with one hand, I drew circles on the dark wood tabletop with the other. "Thank goodness. I can't tell you the sleep I lose over him and whether he's safe at night, but trying to keep track of him—without him feeling like he's being kept track of—makes him anxious. So I try not to be the overprotective parent."

We grew silent after that, all of us eating our dinner amidst the noise and music of the dinner crowd, but I couldn't stop thinking about Sister Patricia.

"I'm worried about Sister Patricia, Higgs. She may be crotchety, but she's not superhuman. How long do you think before she crumbles under the pressure of jail? She's lived a cloistered life, for pity's sake."

"Not so cloistered she wasn't capable of committing a carnal sin, Trixie," Coop reminded, taking an enormous bite of her favorite burger and munching happily.

"Now, now, Coop. Let he who is without sin cast the first stone," I warned. "Not everything is black and white. There's always some gray."

What Sister Patricia had done was wrong—so wrong—but to condemn wasn't our place. Not at this point in time. We didn't know her reasoning behind indulging in an affair of the flesh, and we couldn't speculate.

Coop's matter-of-fact look shot daggers at me. "I only speak the truth. If leading a life of honesty is important, I'm doing my best to keep things honest."

Higgs gave her one of his infamous grins of approval. "You tell her, Coop."

She looked back at him. "I just did. Are your ears working, Cross Higglesworth?"

We burst out laughing. But then I remembered Sister Ophelia's iPad in my purse, and I knew I had to share the information with Higgs.

"When I'm done here, I have to stop at the police station and give something to Tansy."

He cocked his head. "As in hell, for not texting you back about Sister Patricia's questioning?"

I laughed as I gathered up our napkins and put them on my tray. "No, silly. Sister Rita stopped by the shop today and brought me Sister Ophelia's iPad."

He sipped at his beer, eyeing me over the rim of the mug filled with amber liquid. "Because you're her niece?"

I made a face at him and lobbed one of my crumpled napkins at his head. "Look, I'm just trying to catch a killer, okay? Sometimes you have to get in the mud for the greater good."

Popping the last of his burger in his mouth, he nodded. "Uh-huh. You sure got in the mud. Eyeball deep, Miss Community Service."

Rolling my eyes, I stood up, avoiding the overhead canister light, and leaned over the small wood table to poke him in the arm.

"You don't think I feel enough guilt already for telling like a hundred lies in a row to, of all people, a holy woman? I'm an ex-nun. Guilt is my specialty, buddy, but I think I like instilling it better than feeling it."

Pulling on his light jacket, Higgs took the last sip of his beer and rose, too. "Hey, listen. I don't want you two to walk to the station alone—in case Sister Patricia isn't responsible for the headless guy. So, why don't you two come with me to the church first, and then I'll go with. I just want to take a quick peek in on Father Rico and see how he's doing."

"Oh, that would be lovely. I can't believe I didn't think of that. I'm so caught up in my suspect-less investigation, I forgot all about how terrible he must be feeling, especially when we've had no word about what's happening with Sister Patricia. I'm happy to go with you, Higgs."

Coop patted Higgs on the shoulder. "Me, too, Higgs. I love Father Rico. He's kind, and I don't like thinking about someone as kind as him being sad. He should always be happy. Also, did you know it's Deacon Delacorte's birthday today? I heard Mrs. Henry say she was going to bring him cupcakes. He's fifty-six today, and I'd like to wish him a happy birthday if he's still there."

"*Fifty-six*? Wow. I hope I look that good when I'm fifty-six," I joked. "I didn't peg him for a day over thirty-five. Do you suppose it's the sacrament keeping him looking so young?"

Higgs groaned. "I guess I have to give it to you there. He's dreamier than even I gave him credit for."

I giggled, but Coop cocked her head. "I don't know what that means. I only know the sound of his voice makes me happy, and he's very nice."

Higgs grinned at her. "Are you happy, Coop?" he asked, and I suppose it was a valid question, considering she still couldn't smile.

"Duh," she said, pulling the sides of her mouth upward. "This is my happy face."

He laughed at her. "Then let's do this," Higgs said, wending his way through the tiny shop with its wooden benches and tightly packed-in people.

The rain had begun in earnest again, making us pick up our pace. As it pelted my head and we hopped over the rugged sidewalk, I thought about how helpless Sister Patricia must feel right now, and my heart clenched.

Don't get me wrong, I'm no fan of hers, per se. She was

always quite curt with me, especially after she found out I was shunned by my convent. I suppose I could feel petty about that in a how-dare-she-cast-aspersions-when-she-broke-her-vows-way-worse-than-I-ever-could kind of way. I'd only mooned some of my fellow sisters. I hadn't committed a carnal sin.

But I didn't. I felt a bone-deep sadness because I was almost certain she had nothing to do with this or, if she did, that horrible Mr. Coletti had manipulated her. He was a divorce lawyer, after all. It's not as though he didn't know how to manipulate someone and win the game. I'd love to see this ironclad prenup Mrs. Coletti talked about, and what exactly he thought was worth protecting by killing someone.

Either way, I was convinced Sister Patricia was innocent and not nearly as tough as she'd have some of the children she taught believe.

How would a nun survive in jail? They'd eat her alive. The horrible images of her suffering someone named Big Lu were surfing around the edges of my brain, and they wouldn't stop.

I was so lost in my train of thought, I didn't see the pothole on the sidewalk, and in an attempt to avoid the people in front of me, I stepped to the right—and fell right into a gaping hole.

"Oh!" I yelped, wincing as I almost crumpled to the ground.

Higgs grabbed me just in time, but I'd still managed to twist my ankle but good. "Hey, you okay?"

I tried to put pressure on it, but it stung like a you know what. "Shoot," I whimpered. "I'm sorry, Higgs. I think I might have twisted it."

He reached down and rubbed my very tender ankle as it quickly began to swell, making me wince harder. Of all the stupid luck. "It's starting to swell up," he said, as I hobbled around on one foot. "Doesn't feel like you broke anything, but you might want to go to the ER just in case."

I protested in the way of a groan. "I'm not going to the ER for a sprained ankle. It'll take a hundred years to see a doctor for him to charge me hundreds more just to tell me something I already know."

Coop looked at me over Higgs's back, the rain soaking her beautiful hair, leaving it plastered to her skull. She held the flashlight from her phone over my foot and frowned with a hiss.

"Trixie, we need to ice that."

Higgs bent his knees and crouched in front of me as Coop helped hold me up. "Okay, it's settled. On my back. I'll piggyback you to the church, we'll get you an ice pack, and we'll take my car to the station afterward."

"It's not that bad," I protested as the rain began to seep through my sweater and I spat to keep it from getting into my mouth.

"Well, let's not take any chances, huh? Get on, Trixie. C'mon, it's pouring out."

With a sigh, I let Coop help me hop onto Higgs's back, wrapping my arms around his neck as my foot throbbed.

He gripped my legs and said, "Hold tight. I'm gonna make a break for it. Coop, you with me?"

She slapped him on the shoulder. "Right behind you."

Oh, sometimes I could just laugh at some of the

ironic things Higgs said unknowingly. Was she with him? She could outrun him before he'd even blinked an eye.

Instead, I tucked my head into the back of his neck and tried not to outwardly sniff his hair because even wet, it smelled good.

All of him smelled good, and his broad back was a lot broader pressed to the front of me.

As he bobbed and weaved through the few people out walking, lightly jogging toward the church, my ankle began to really pound. I was relieved when I finally saw the church and he took the steps without missing a beat.

Coop propped the door open to let us through, the warmth inside instantly greeting me as Higgs carefully set me down on the floor and helped me hobble to a pew.

I have to admit, I was a little flustered after clinging to his back. Flustered and feeling all manner of butterflies in the pit of my belly, but I think I did a good job of covering my breathlessness when I smiled up at him.

"Thanks, Higgs," I said, fighting my shyness.

He smiled down at me, his dark hair soaked, his black jacket covered in fat splotches of rain. "You bet. Now stay put. Don't try and walk on that or you might make it worse. I'll go check on Father Rico and get some ice for that ankle, okay?"

I nodded, pulling my phone out of my back pocket. "You got it."

Coop gripped my shoulder. "Do you mind if I go with him, Trixie?"

"Nope. Scoot, the both of you. I'm just going to handle some emails for the shop while I wait. Go-go!" I ordered with a grin as they both scurried toward the back of the church to find Father Rico.

Looking over the long row of pews toward the pulpit, seeing the beauty of the candles lining the steps, and the gorgeous stands of flowers bracketing the altar, I sighed.

The peace resonated with me in a way I'd ignored since I left Saint Aloysius By The Sea. There were so many aspects of being a faithful servant of the church that I missed, and this truly was one of them. The quiet whisper of the joy I'd once reveled in slipped into my heart, and I closed my eyes and relished the moment with a deep inhale.

The ping of my phone disturbed that, and it had me fumbling to click on my texts. A chill raced up my spine when I realized it was from Tansy.

Some information on the headless corpse found at Our Lady. Not much, but thought you'd like to know we have but one small clue. A pack of matches from a restaurant in China. Yes, you read that right. China. Coroner found it in a hidden pocket sewn inside the victim's pants, along with a fifty dollar bill. Busy as a bee here. Be back with you shortly.

I texted her back as quickly as I could and asked after Sister Patricia, but those infuriating three dots, indicating she was texting back, went away and didn't show back up again.

I clenched my fists and fought a scream. When I finally got my hands on her, I was going to give her the old what for. I realize we'd made a deal, and she said she'd feed me information as she saw fit, but Christmas alive, she was killing me with her dribs and drabs.

I needed to know how Sister Patricia was, for gravy's sake.

DAKOTA CASSIDY

Looking down at my phone, I reread her text. Matches from a restaurant in China...huh. How bizarre. And who had an inside pocket in their pants?

Frustrated, I decided to watch a little of *Unsolved Mysteries* in order to feel closer to Sister Ophelia. Being here in the church, going over and over what happened, was driving me nuts and ruining the peace I'd felt moments ago. Plus, my foot ached like a son of a gun. I needed a distraction while I waited for Coop and Higgs.

What was it again? Season twelve, episode ten. Clicking on the episode, I grimaced at how tiny my phone's screen was. Robert Stack appeared, a man Sister Ophelia once told me, had he knocked on her door and asked her to run away with him, she'd do so, lickety-split.

I'd laughed and laughed when she'd shared that, and already the memory had me smiling, despite the horror of the episode featuring a man named Emile Franklin, wanted in connection to the 1997 kidnapping, torture, and murder of an oil tycoon from Oklahoma by the name of Roscoe Wyatt.

They'd found Roscoe's dismembered body in a silo on a farm in Idaho, but only after Emile Franklin's partner, Paxton Raye gave up the location of the body and that Emile had been his accomplice.

However, Emile was still at large as of the time of the broadcast, which put this crime's timestamp at sometime in the nineties. But the really scary part? The pair were both twenty-two at the time they'd pulled off the crime, and they'd snatched Roscoe right from his bed where he'd been sound asleep.

The motivation? Money. "Duh," I murmured to Robert

176

Stack. It was the root of all evil. They'd wanted five million in ransom for his safe return.

Except, Roscoe's only living relative, his son, Garth Wyatt, refused to pay it. Apparently, there was no love lost between father and son.

Yikes.

Sister Ophelia had some pretty gruesome nighttime viewing. Not that I didn't watch things of this nature, too. I was just surprised Sister O watched it before bed. She was a tough old bird, I'll give her that.

As the picture of the remaining fugitive of the law flashed across the screen, I was impressed with how clear it was. Most of them were so grainy, you couldn't tell who it was even if it turned out to be your next-door neighbor, but this one was clear as day. I pressed pause to study it, but I couldn't put my finger on why I found it so fascinating.

Also, I hate to admit it, him being a killer and all, but he sure was a looker. Dark, tan, tall, built like a linebacker.

I blinked.

Wait.

Sister Ophelia had been watching this *before* she went to the speed-dating event. I knew that for sure because of Sister Rita. At the speed-dating event, she'd had something important she wanted to talk to Father Rico about, but never had the opportunity because he'd been too wrapped up in his duties as host.

The episode she'd been watching featured a guy who was good-looking and, according to this broadcast from 1999, would now be forty-four years old.

I gulped as I stared at the picture on my phone. This

must have been the "something important" she'd wanted to discuss with Father Rico.

In fact, it would also explain why she was stress-smoking the afternoon of the speed-dating event, when I'd seen her by the dumpster. She had, quite by chance, discovered a wanted killer, on the run for over twenty-two years.

A killer who looked just like—

"Evening, Trixie. Can I help with something?"

eacon Delacorte. He looked just like Deacon Delacorte.

Oh. Gravy.

In that moment, much like all the moments just before I figured out the identity of a killer, all the information I'd been gathering or had heard up to that point rushed into my brain, smooshing facts together against more facts until they all came at me in one tidal wave of startling clarity.

Now I understood why Artur had drawn a television. He wasn't trying to show me a TV, per se. He'd tried to lead me to the *TV* show, *Unsolved Mysteries*. Understanding how and why he'd done that was for another time.

For now…

Why, universe, why, oh why, do you wait until the eleventh hour to give me the gift of sight?

Deacon Delacorte wasn't the real Deacon Delacorte back from a peace mission in China, and he sure wasn't fifty-six. Not even. He couldn't be, because he was, in fact, Emile Franklin, now forty-four.

And listen, don't hate me for saying this because he's a super-bad guy, but I promise you, he doesn't look a day over thirty-five. A life of crime hasn't aged him even a little.

Couple that with the fact that we had a fingerprint-less, unidentified body on our hands and Roscoe Wyatt had been found in a similar condition, and I had a theory...for all it's worth at this heightened moment of fear.

Sister Ophelia recognized fake Deacon Delacorte on *Unsolved Mysteries*, she was going to tattle on him, which was what got her strangled.

Why she simply hadn't gone to the police instead of waiting to talk to Father Rico was a question I might never have an answer for.

Fake Deacon Delacorte must have killed the *real* Davis Delacorte, stolen his identity and, to prevent the body from being identified, burned his fingerprints off and hacked off his head. Not that it mattered, because the headless body had given him up.

Know how I know who the body in the closet is?

China. That's how.

The real Deacon Delacorte had just returned from China, and the body in the church closet had a pack of matches from a Chinese restaurant in a secret pocket sewn into the inside of his pants.

And of course, the fake Deacon Delacorte had flashed Chinese money at our meeting at the coffee shop earlier today. So not only had he killed the real Deacon Delacorte, he'd stolen his money.

How rude.

But now the question was, why the heck would he put the real deacon's body in the church storage closet anyway?

I mean, hello. Isn't that just inviting disaster to take you out on a date?

"Trixie? Is everything all right?" Deacon Delacorte asked, leaning his hip on the pew, pleasant as could be as he smiled his handsome smile.

Oh, yeah. It's great. Know why? I just put together that you're a cold-blooded killer and you're standing here in front of me with your cold-blooded killer smile, and I have to pretend like nothing's wrong.

Yep. I'm right as rain.

My heart began to pound so hard in my chest, I was sure he'd hear my sheer terror and panic in its rhythm. Holy Hannah, I'd better keep it together and act like nothing was wrong, or I'd be dead in the water.

And where the heck were Coop and Higgs, anyway? How long did it take to check on Father Rico? I felt exposed and caught before I'd actually been accused of anything.

My clammy hands clung to my phone as I tried to find the button to click the screen off, but I managed a slow nod.

"Oh, I'm fine, Deacon Delacorte. Just waiting for Higgs and Coop. They're checking on Father Rico. He was so distraught earlier today, we thought we should do a quick mental health check."

Yeah. That sounded good to my ears. My voice didn't shake and I smiled almost the entire time.

"Why aren't you with them then?" he asked, cocking his head and leaning in close—close enough that I could smell his cologne.

A nice scented mix of springtime and musky woods, if you must know.

When he leaned farther into me, I noticed something

else—the final nail in his coffin, so to speak. His stole, a vestment he still wore from afternoon mass and the color purple for Lent, had a burn mark on the underside.

A round burn—likely a cigarette burn from his struggle with Sister Ophelia.

But I clung to my fight to stay calm. I held up my foot to show him, which had grown fat and ugly as I'd sat and neglected to elevate.

"Twisted my ankle on the way over. Fell in a pothole, of all things. I'm sooo clumsy sometimes, I could just cry. It was too hard to walk, so I plopped a squat here to wait for them."

His brow furrowed—his smooth, unlined, not-fifty-six-at-all brow. "Oh no. Let me take a peek." Davis leaned down and reached for my leg, but I jumped, and I jumped so fast, I even scared myself.

"*No!*" I cried out, cringing at his attempt to touch me before I lowered my voice and clenched my hands together around my phone. "Sorry. It just *really* hurts."

In that very brief second, when he appeared as though he were working something out in his mind, I somehow un-paused *Unsolved Mysteries.* Probably because I was shaking so hard.

As is the way of my luck, Robert Stack was in the middle of repeating the name of Deacon Delacorte's, a.k.a. Emile Franklin's victim, and if he'd used a megaphone, with the help of the acoustics in the church, it couldn't have been any louder.

That was the moment the jig was up. I knew it. I saw it—and so did he.

He snaked a hand out and grabbed my ankle, wrapping

his incredibly strong fingers around it and squeezing with such brute force, it brought tears to my eyes.

We looked at each other then. Me, I'm sure, with all the horror and fear of discovery in my wide eyes. Him, with a narrowed gaze that burned holes in my face.

Then he squeezed tighter, clenching his teeth with the effort. "Does that hurt, Trixie?"

I swallowed hard, fighting the sting of tears. *"Please let me go,"* I whimpered.

"I'm sorry it hurts, Trixie," he said with a cold, empty smile that never reached his eyes. "I hate the idea that you might be in any pain—*ever*." Upon those words, he yanked my leg, pulling me from the pew with such a vicious tug, I fell backward and hit my head on the hard wood. My hip popped; leaving me more than surprised he hadn't dislocated my limb.

The burn of my ankle, coupled with the agonizing white-hot heat of my abused leg, made it hard to focus on what to do next.

So I cried out instead. "Deacon Delacorte! *What are you doing?*" I screamed, gripping the edge of the seat of the pew for all I was worth to keep from being dragged.

He stopped for only a moment. "Oh, Trixie," he rumbled, still as pleasant as he'd been since the day I'd first met him. "I think you know what I'm doing. Or what I'm going to do —to *you*, that is."

Deacon Delacorte was stronger than I'll ever be, because he yanked again, making me cry out at the stabbing pain in my swollen ankle. His face remained placid and determined as he dragged me from the pew and into the aisle.

When he began hauling me toward the front of the

church's vestibule, it was with almost no effort at all. I'm not a skinny girl by any stretch of the imagination, but you'd think I was nothing more than a wet noodle with the way he hauled me across the hard floor, scraping my back and stretching my leg till I thought it would snap.

His grip on my ankle was made of steel, but I tried kicking at him with my other foot anyway.

"Stop! You don't want to do this! I already told the police who you are, *Emile Franklin*!"

That stopped him dead to rights. He went completely motionless, turning around to look at me as my chest heaved, and I tried to sit up on my elbows to stare him down.

But he didn't appear at all afraid I'd called him out. In fact, for someone who was teetering on the edge of being caught after being on the run for twenty-two years, he was remarkably unruffled.

And that scared me more than any other killer I'd come in this kind of contact with so far.

He wasn't at all fearful of the notion I'd really called the police. In seconds, I found out why. Emile Franklin stared me down with his suddenly soulless black eyes and whispered menacingly, "You didn't call the police, Trixie. Know how I know?"

I gulped, forcing saliva into my mouth so I could speak. "H…how?"

"I just heard Coop and your boyfriend tell Father Rico they had to get back to you, because you wanted to bring Sister Ophelia's *iPad* to the police."

My heart nosedived to my feet and my pulse throbbed in

my ears. "But they don't even know what I found. Please! I'm begging you, don't hurt them!"

He gave me a scathing grin, full of a psychopath's special brand of twisted malice. "But it wouldn't have been long until they found out what you know, Trixie, would it? Because I know all about you. Yes, I do. You would have told them the second they left Father Rico's office. I couldn't let you do that and I couldn't let *them* do that either. You don't know how to leave things alone, and I knew if you hadn't already, you'd figure it out eventually. Or at the very least, you'd take it to the police and they'd figure it out—and I was right, wasn't I?"

Fear coursed through my veins, making my blood run cold. Shoot. This reputation I had for sticking my nose into a crime didn't always work in my favor, because he was right.

Emile gave me a knowing look then. "See? I knew it. Just like Sister Ophelia. She had the same look on her face as you do. She found out, too, you know. I heard her tell Father Rico she had to talk to him. That's why I followed her outside. I knew something was wrong from the second she saw me when she arrived at the speed-dating event. And if I didn't know then, I would have known when she realized we were alone outside. Everyone gives me that same look when they recognize me from that stupid, stupid show. That look of pure terror and disgust they can't hide no matter how hard they try—and you know what that means, don't you?"

"What?"

"It means *I have to kill them*," he rasped. "It means I have to eliminate *any* possible chance someone might put it all together. Like Sister Ophelia. Like your friends. Like *you.*"

I blinked, trying to sit up as more ice ran through my veins and his words sank in. He'd said *everyone* gave him that same look of pure terror.

Which meant…

Licking my lips, I asked, "Wait! What do you mean by 'everyone'? You've killed other people for recognizing you from *Unsolved Mysteries?*"

Emile winked and flashed a toothy, white grin. "Aw, sure, Trixie. At least two, and I'll keep right on killing them if they keep cropping up. No way am I going to end up like that dipstick Paxton. Doing a life sentence, even after he gave me up! I ask you, what kind of deal was that?"

As a side note, wowzers, huh? I guess the show really had been instrumental in catching fugitives. I was never sure if they plumped their stats for ratings or they really did catch a lot of criminals.

As another revelation came to me, I tried to do two things at once. Figure out how to get away from him with a bum ankle and leg and find out why he'd done this.

My arms shook, trying to keep me propped up, my stomach muscles ached, but I *needed* to hear him confess.

"So you strangled her with your vestment, didn't you? That's how you got that hole in it."

He used one hand to lift up the purple stole and shrugged his shoulders with another dazzling smile. "Niiice work, Trixie. You're really not half bad at this, *Miss Marple…*" he taunted.

I almost gagged on my next question, but for some

sadistic reason, I had to hear it anyway. "So was that the real Deacon Delacorte in the storage closet?"

He sighed dramatically, mocking my question. "Yeeeah."

"Why?" I croaked, straining with everything I had to stay upright. "*Why him?*"

"I was high and dry, Trixie. Someone had tipped off the FBI about seeing me in Wyoming. I needed somewhere safe to hide. That I ran into Deacon Delacorte at a diner here in Cobbler Cove was pure dumb luck. Luckier still when I heard him tell the waitress he was just back from China after some religious journey garbage, and on his way to meet his new congregation. I mean, I was raised by two religious nuts in the Catholic church. I knew everything I needed to know to step right into the role of deacon. So I made an executive decision."

"But doesn't he have family? People who know him? People who'd know you weren't him? Pictures of him in China?"

Nodding his head, he grinned. "That's the icing on the cake. To make everything that much sweeter, he's an *orphan*, and most all of the people he spent the better part of his adult life with are in China. I heard him tell his waitress. Went on ad nauseam about it. Also, we looked a lot alike. Enough that I could have pulled it off with ease. That made everything perfect. *Perfect*. It was everything I needed to start a new life that would last more than a few stupid months, and no one would have ever known he wasn't me. I had a fake ID made and I just stepped into his identity. Easy-peasy. It's hard when you're on the run for so long. This was a sign, Trixie. *A sign from God,*" he whispered, the echo of his voice swishing through the building.

A killer who needed a place to call home. Yikes.

Goose bumps covered my arms and raised the hair on the back of my neck. "But why, of all the places in the world, after killing him, would you leave his body in the storage closet?"

I wanted to call him an idiot for doing that, but I suppose, in the position I was in, I'd end up dead a lot quicker if I incited him. Plus, he'd eluded the FBI and the local police for over two decades. Who was the real idiot here?

Rolling his gorgeous eyes, Emile exhaled long and loud. "I couldn't leave him in the my refrigerator forever, could I? But yeah, I'll admit, that was a dumb mistake on my part. Yes, Trixie, even calculated killers like me screw up. All I had to do was carry his body from my apartment in the back, where I'd stored him while I figured out what to do with him, to the side of the church where my car—er, *Deacon Delacorte's* car is parked. But as you know, there's only one way to get from my attached apartment out back to the side entrance. I stupidly thought the church would be empty. But wouldn't you know, that octopus of a woman Carla showed up with her big mouth and her happy hands. So I ducked into the closet and dumped him. I just couldn't seem to get away from her long enough to get him the hell out of there and, well...you know the rest."

Disgust made my stomach turn at the callous disregard he had for the real Deacon Delacorte and what he'd done to him, so much disgust I had to fight vomiting.

"So you beheaded him and burned his fingerprints off to keep the police from identifying him?" I squeaked, even though I already knew the answer. I was just trying to buy some time to do something—*anything.*

He winked with a playful chuckle. "I did. Does that frighten you, Trixie?"

"Well, on the one hand," I grunted as my arms refused to hold me up anymore and I fell to the hard floor. "It's not exactly comforting to know my head's going to end up somewhere the rest of me isn't. But on the other, I won't know that, will I?"

"You know, Trixie, you have an amazing attitude," he commended with a cluck of his tongue. "Which is why I guess you were a nun. I wish we'd had more than the few days we did to get to know one another. I sure like you." Then he turned away as though he were going to begin dragging me again.

"Wait! Wait! I have some advice. Do yourself a favor. Make sure to check my clothing before you hack me up."

"*What?*" he asked.

"The real Deacon Delacorte's body still had pants on, and inside the pants he had a secret pocket sewn. In that pocket, there was a book of matches from a Chinese restaurant *in China.* That's how I put some of this together. And you almost paid for our coffee with Chinese money."

He wiped a hand across his brow. "Phew. Saved by the nun. Thanks, Trixie," he said jovially.

As he turned away and started to drag me the rest of the way, I yelped, "Wait! Just wait. One more thing!"

Emile stopped again and turned back around, giving me a look that said he'd indulge me just this once. "Okay. One more, and then we have to hurry this along. I have a lot of you to dispose of before I get the hell out of here."

I fought a loud gasp because he'd essentially answered my next question, but I asked anyway, and this time, my voice was shaky and my blood ran cold.

"Where are Coop and Higgs? And Father Rico. Did you…did you kill them?"

I closed my eyes and prayed then. Prayed he'd say no.

"Waiting for the same fate as you, Trixie," he said, as if I'd asked a silly question. "You know I can't let them live any more than I can let *you* stay breathing. You all know too much. Now it's time to go."

And without another word, he began to pull me the rest of the way toward the vestibule. But not only was I fueled by hope because he'd said Coop and Higgs were "waiting for the same fate" as me, which I took to mean *alive*. I was fueled by the hope that Coop would say to heck with hiding her strength from Higgs and Father Rico, and bust out of wherever Emile had them—because I was certain he had them stashed somewhere.

While the terror in me, along with my predicament, began to set in, as I clawed at the floor, trying to grab on to the sides of the pews as they rolled by me, my mind whirred with what to do next.

I figured jackknifing upward and catching him by surprise with a roundhouse punch to the face was at best, unlikely. I couldn't jackknife out of bed after a lazy Sunday sleep in, let alone jackknife up off the floor with someone holding my aching ankle in a vise grip.

Tears sprang to my eyes the farther we got; my hands ached and I screamed for him to stop as my frustration level grew, and then everything went quite suddenly,z an insidious black.

CHAPTER 17

"*T*rixie Lavender, you must stop! Stooooop!" Coop screamed.

Like, actually screamed.

It was the first thing I heard, the first thing that was capable of piercing that cloudy haze of my demonic possession. Then there were hands pulling at me, dragging me, pushing me up against a wall so hard, it knocked the breath out of me.

A slap to my cheek cleared my vision. "Look at me, Trixie! Look at me now! Focus on me. It's Coop. You must stop!" she yelled, then lowered her voice and forced me to look into her eyes. "Higgs is here, Trixie. He's *here*."

All at once, as was the norm for one of my demonically possessed outbursts, I went slack, my muscles released, my fists unclenched—and indeed I saw Higgs over Coop's shoulder.

And his face said it all.

"Trixie?" Higgs murmured in abject horror. I heard it in

his voice, saw it in his eyes, and right then and there, I prayed for death.

Yes, that's a sin, in a roundabout way, I suppose, but the way Higgs was looking at me made me feel far dirtier than breaking a commandment ever could.

It was only then that I saw Emile Franklin's battered body on the floor not far from my feet. Obviously, Coop had pulled me off him.

Good heavens, he was a mess. His nose was bloody, his eyes were so black and blue and swollen, I could barely see them. There was a stray tooth but inches from him, and his arm lie crookedly next to his body, clearly broken.

He tried to move, tried to scurry away, but was helpless to do much more than whimper, "Get her away from me! Keep her away from me!"

Oh, dear. I'd really done it this time, eh?

"Shut him up!" Coop ordered, her face hard and unyielding. "Call Tansy, Higgs! Do it now!"

Higgs blinked, his beautiful eyes that once looked at me with warmth and smiles were riddled with disbelief. "But…"

Letting me go, but keeping me near, Coop swung around to face him. "I said call Tansy, Higgs. My phone is broken after the tussle with Deacon Delacorte. So do it. *Now*," she seethed, and I have to admit, she was much better at anger than she was at happiness because even I wanted to call Tansy.

Higgs fumbled with his phone while I looked to Coop for answers. "Tussle?" I rasped, my throat typically raw and hoarse after an outburst.

"Yes. Deacon Delacorte, who I suppose isn't really Deacon Delacorte, tied us up at knifepoint and was going to come back and take us somewhere he could kill us without leaving behind another mess he'd have to clean. I let him, of course because what was I to do? Reveal my strength? Father Rico was so afraid, he passed out cold, but Higgs..." She sighed, her way of showing her frustration. "After the deacon left to go find you, I...well, I untied us. I promise you, Trixie, I tried to hide my strength as best I could, but there was no way I was going to let him kill you. But I promise you, Father Rico didn't see anything."

"Higgs..." I whispered with my own horror, placing a hand over my mouth to keep from crying out.

"Yes," she hissed, gripping my jaw in her hand. "He saw. But he didn't only see me, Trixie. *He saw you.*"

I looked into her eyes, my darkest fear rising to the top of my skull, threatening to cancel out everything and explode from my brain.

"Am I a mess?" was all I could manage.

Coop, never one to mince words, looked me square in the eye. "Like you went ten rounds in a cage fight and just barely got out alive."

The moment she said that was the moment all feeling returned to my nerve endings. Everything, and I do mean even my eyelashes, *hurt*.

I lifted my hands to see my knuckles were shredded. And upon looking down, I saw my clothes were covered in blood spatter. My earlier ankle sprain began to hurt so much, I didn't think I could stand on it any longer.

"My face?" I asked, because if my hands were any indication of the fight, my face was probably worse.

Coop pushed my hair from my eyes and used her thumb to wipe something from the side of my mouth. "Also a mess.

You have two black eyes and a split lip. He must have tried to fight back. But you showed *him*, because he's worse."

I groaned when I heard police sirens bleat out their warning. "How can I explain?"

She gripped me by the caps of my shoulders and gave me a slight shake. "Let me handle this, Trixie. Please trust I can handle this."

Finally able to lift my arms, I pulled her into my embrace in weak relief. "Thank God you're okay. I was so afraid for you and Higgs."

Higgs stood on the peripheral of the scene, his face still rich with disbelief. It was as though he was afraid to come near me, and who could blame him? I'm certain he'd witnessed a monster.

The rush of police and the sound of Tansy's voice had Coop giving me a quick squeeze before disentangling my arms from her neck and propping me against the wall. "Stay here, Trixie. I promise, I'll handle this."

My stomach recoiled then, the urge to vomit my dinner almost stronger than the urge to pass out. Someone helped me to a chair in the vestibule. One of the only ones not smashed to bits courtesy of me, I suppose.

Tansy barked orders and sent the paramedics to me. They patched me up as best they could with ice packs and bandages and, while they weren't sure if I needed stitches, a strong recommendation to visit the ER was given.

But all I could do was think about what *Higgs* must be thinking. How he must have felt, seeing me that way.

"Love? Look at me." Tansy said, kneeling in front of me and tilting my chin upward with her hand. "You're wrecked, Miss Marple. That must have been some fight."

My eyes filled with tears, and my heart nearly burst. "I—"

"No, no. Don't tell me your version now. Coop explained everything I need to know for the moment. You just rest and come in tomorrow to make a statement, yes?"

I looked at her through my swollen eyes as tears fell down my cheeks. "Really?"

She smiled warmly, sympathetically. "Of course, love. You need to go to the hospital first. I can't have my best unofficial copper in anything but tip-top condition. We've got this now. Though, I can't imagine you'll tell me anything different than Higgs and Coopie did. Really, all I need is your signature on an official statement, and that surely can wait. Now, go get yourself a warm cuppa. Bet Father Rico has some in his office. The rest will sit." She gave my arm a gentle squeeze and was gone.

Coop rushed in just as they carried Emile Franklin out on a stretcher while he cried out and pointed at me, "She's crazy! Get her away from me!"

"C'mon. Let's go get some of that tea, Trixie Lavender. Higgs is waiting in Father Rico's office."

But I tried to dig my heels in and stop her from forcing me to see Higgs. "No! I can't, Coop. I can't!"

"You can and you will. You will not leave him like some cliffhanger, wondering if he saw what you darn well know he saw. I won't let you. I'm ever so glad I saw *Dynasty* long after it was on television, or I might have had a rage-filled fit, waiting until the next season. Now buck up, Sister Trixie. It's time to get this handled once and for all."

"You mean tell him the truth?" I squealed, gripping her upper arm.

"That's exactly what I mean. Now, put your arm around my neck and let me help you. I'm tired of deceiving someone I care so much about. I trust Higgs. Once he's past the shock, he'll either accept us or not. But no more hiding from the people closest to us."

As she helped me hobble down the long hall to Father Rico's office, my heart crashed against my ribs and my head buzzed with the million and one explanations. Even after she pushed open Father Rico's heavy office door, my brain was still whirring.

Until Higgs's head popped up and he saw me.

Then I wanted to curl into a ball and lie down and die.

"Trixie…" He hummed my name, his voice still full of disbelief. Disbelief that turned to fear. I saw it—tasted it—felt it in every crevice, every nerve ending.

So I held up a hand, fighting hot tears. "Higgs. Please listen—"

He backed away, setting down the cup of tea he'd been preparing, but Coop was quick to step between my raw, beaten body and Higgs's disbelief.

"Cross Higglesworth, this is going to take some explaining and a certain amount of stretching your beliefs and maybe even your imagination. Please, before you become anxious and fearful, you must *listen*. I insist you do us the courtesy of listening."

But Higgs kept backing away and shaking his head, his usually tanned face gone pale and chalky. He held up a finger as his mouth began to open and his head kept shaking.

"No…no. I…*no*," he murmured, his eyes far away and glassy.

Coop approached him and gripped him by the shoulders and, from the look of shock on his handsome face, she was using a decent amount of force. With a face hard enough to crack a walnut, she looked him directly in the eye, her jaw clenching.

"I must insist you sit down and listen to me—to *us*, Cross Higglesworth. I hold you in high regard, but I will not hesitate to force my will upon you if you do not sit and listen to what we have to tell you. And please don't think for one minute I *can't* force you to my will. *I can*. I don't like the notion. But I can. *I will*."

Tears began to spill from my eyes as I heard Coop order Higgs to stay put. I think I'd always known this day would come; I just hadn't ever planned on it coming so soon. I'd rehearsed a million scenarios in my head. I'd prepared a million speeches to explain what Higgs had just witnessed.

But they'd all been distant and muted words until now, and my frustration, my fear of being found out, Higgs's wide-eyed disbelief, the horror all over his handsome face, all came crashing down around my ears.

Seeing me that way, violent and raging, had to be an ugly experience, even for an ex-undercover cop who'd seen more violence than most. And I hated it. I hated that he'd seen me behave like a rabid animal, frothing at the mouth and struggling against Coop, who literally was the only person who could contain me.

But there was no going back now. If I had any hope of salvaging this friendship we'd built, one on the precipice of something more substantial, he deserved to know who I truly was.

And if he walked away, I'd hurt for the rest of my life

because of it. He might put a pin of dissolution in my bubble, but I'd live. As sad as that would make me, I'd manage.

I'd lost before and come out all right on the other end. I'd do it again if need be, if this was just too much for him to handle.

"*Higgs,*" Coop warned, her raspy voice hissing against the walls of Father Rico's office. "Will you listen?"

I know Higgs pretty well, but the one thing I can't ever say I've seen in his chocolate-brown eyes is horror. He's been fearful in his very stoic sort of way, he's been surprised, hurt, but never horrified—and each time he looked at me, he was just that.

Horrified.

I knew his mind was whizzing with possibilities for what he'd just witnessed, trying to absorb and parse my vile behavior, but he couldn't, and it left him stupefied.

Keeping my hands at my side, I fisted them and hobbled to him with caution. From past experience, I knew my hair was a rat's nest of a mess, my eyes were likely bloodshot and red rimmed, and my face streaked with tears.

Add in the certainty of bruises from my fight with Emile Franklin, and I probably looked pretty scary. So I went with caution, and he continued to back up as far as he could without actually climbing out the window.

Bracing my hands on Father Rico's desk, I looked him in the eye. "Higgs," I whispered, my throat raw from the screaming I hear I always do when Artur takes over. "I know you're afraid, but I need you to hear me. Please just hear what I have to say. *Please.*"

Higgs blinked then, the fringe of his lashes sweeping his

cheeks as he leaned back against the wall. His body language said he wanted nothing to do with me, but I saw his head and his heart war with the notion.

That's when he held up a hand and finally addressed me, his words contained, measured, his jaw tight and clenched. "I want to say I'll *always* listen to you, Trixie. I never thought that would ever change…but I'm going to be as honest as I can right now and try to maintain some piece of my sanity. I don't know what I'm capable of actually hearing, or if I can absorb what you're going to say. But I want to, Trixie. *I. Want. To.*"

I gulped and inhaled, closing my eyes. "That's all I ask is that you listen. What I'm going to tell you is going to sound absurd, bananapants crazy—like straight out of some horror movie. But I swear as I stand here before you, in a house of the Lord, it's *all true*. Every word I'm about to share is all the truth. *My truth.*"

He looked at me for a long time, and I managed to hold his gaze without crumbling…and then he held out a hand to me.

I reached over the desk, my hand visibly trembling, and I took his and clung, letting his warm skin sear mine.

And then I began.

~

*H*iggs blinked and inhaled a ragged breath before he spoke, leaning back in the chair he'd finally had to sit in or fall over from shock.

"So let me get this straight. Coop is a *demon*. A demon

who saved you from being dragged through a portal to Hell while she, herself, escaped from Hell."

I swallowed hard. "Yes."

"And Livingston, the *talking* owl, latched on to her when she escaped from Hell, and he's a nice Irish boy trapped in some road kill's body."

"Correct," Coop said, leaning her hip against the desk. "Well, he's mostly nice. Sometimes he tells fake news."

Higgs looked at her, his mouth half open. But then he appeared to gather his thoughts and said, "And Jeff—*my* Jeff —who I thought was a stray, also escaped from Hell and landed in the body of a puppy. He sniffed the two of you out and found you here in Cobbler Cove, and he can talk, too."

I gulped on a wince, my throat tight and dry. "Also correct."

"And *you*," he muttered. "You've been possessed by a demon named Artur, who's responsible for getting you booted from your former convent by controlling your body, and he's the one who turned you into the Hulk tonight."

Closing my eyes, I fought my fear and nodded once more. "Yes."

Then we all fell silent while he reabsorbed what he'd already been trying so desperately to absorb.

I have to give it to Higgs. He'd been quiet, he'd been open to hearing what Coop and I had to say. He hadn't once asked for a break while we spilled our guts, nor had he been at all judgmental. His expression had remained passive the entire time.

And now this—this silence, this waiting on tenterhooks to see his reaction.

"Cross Higglesworth?" Coop said, peering down into his

face. "Are you absorbing? I suggest you absorb quickly so we can take Trixie to the emergency room. I worry her ankle is broken."

But I jumped up and wiped my clammy palms on my aching thighs. As Higgs absorbed, I became increasingly uncomfortable. Telling him our story without actually begging him to accept me left me almost angry. I felt almost judged, which is a natural defense mechanism whether real or imagined.

I didn't ask for this. I didn't invite this chaos into my body. It happened. For lack of a better term, I wasn't going to be victim-blamed because it had.

And that made me unusually snippy. "Listen. You do you, Higgs. Figure this out however you like. Sit with it, think about it, call me if you have questions. But know this —I am who I am. I can't change what's happened, and despite this outlandish story, despite the fact that I have a demon inside me, just waiting to eat my soul, I'm a good person. Everything I've told you is the truth. So, there's nothing left to say, is there?"

"Trixie Lavender!" Coop actually almost yelled, placing her hand on my shoulder and forcing me to sit back down in the chair opposite Higgs's. "Don't become contrary because you're frustrated with Higgs not reacting the way you'd wish. We can't control others' feelings, we can only control our own. Now, please sit down."

There's nothing like having your words thrown back at you, is there? Contrite, I repositioned myself, catching a glimpse of Higgs's surprised face.

Holding up my hands, I acknowledged the truth of Coop's words. "Okay. I'm a little on edge. I apologize. But put yourself in my shoes. I just told another human being I'm *possessed*. I've never done that before."

"So Goose and Knuckles don't know?" Higgs asked as he turned to face me.

"No. The only other people on the planet who know are an ex-witch named Stevie and…" I stopped myself from saying anything else.

The existence of demons was enough for one night. He didn't need to know about my ex-witch/medium friend, her talking bat familiar, her ghostly British spy and the afterlife.

That was for another day.

"Stevie being the woman you stayed with in Ebenezer Falls, where you ran into your first murder, right?"

"Yes," I replied stiffly.

"She's an *ex-witch*?"

"That's another conversation."

"I'll say," he drawled. "So what just happened, the way you went ballistic on Deacon Delacorte or whoever he really is—"

"Emile Franklin."

Higgs cocked his head. "Right. *Him*. All that rage—all that violence—that was because of the demon you harbor? You have no control over it?"

I looked back down at my thighs again, my ankle throbbing to beat the band. "No. I have no control. I typically don't even know when it's going to happen, or that it's happening at all. The attacks are sudden and they're almost always violent, and Coop, being a demon herself, is usually the only one who can settle me because she's so strong. But my last attack was months ago. During the thing with Dr. Fabrizio and Detective Griswald."

He blinked his eyes and ran a hand through his hair. "I have a bazillion questions."

"I bet you do."

"Are you willing to answer them or are you going to snipe at me because I want to understand and that's probably going to annoy you at some point?"

"I'll try not to snipe."

But Coop pushed off of Father Rico's desk and stood between us, holding up a slender hand. "Now that you've heard the worst of this, the rest will have to wait. Trixie's face is blowing up like a balloon and her ankle needs to be checked. No more talking until later," she ordered, holding her hand out to me and gently pulling me upward.

"I'll get the car," he offered…and then he dropped a gentle kiss on my forehead and smiled.

The Higgs smile.

The dazzling one that made my toes curl and my heart race.

Maybe this wouldn't be so bad after all.

EPILOGUE

*E*leven hours, a broken ankle, two black eyes, ten stitches, two sprained fingers and an award made by the ER staff fashioned out of a face mask and some Depends for the baddest ex-nun in the land, later…

*W*e sat on a bench outside the hospital while Coop went and dug the car out of some distant parking lot, me exhausted, Higgs still bursting with questions as though he'd just found out Santa Clause was real.

"So my dog can talk? *Seriously*? Full-sentences, conversation-worthy talk?"

I yawned, even though it hurt to open my mouth that far. "Yes. He has an accent, too. I think his human form was originally from Boston."

"Hah!" Higgs yelped, handing me the coffee he'd gone and found while I was being stitched up. "Do you think he'll talk to me, too?"

"I think if he knows he can talk out in the open freely, he'd talk to Satan."

Higgs nudged my shoulder. "Well, hasn't he already?"

I stifled a small giggle and closed my tired eyes. "Look at you, already in acceptance mode. But truthfully, I don't know. Though, I guess you could ask, right? The whole Satan thing is still something I haven't quite digested as *real*-real, you know what I mean? Like, Coops tells me things, and my jaw hits the floor, and I'm all manner of shocked and in awe. Then disbelief strikes, yet I can't deny her information is real when I have a demon inside me, and she's proven *she's* a demon."

"Yeah." He grew quiet for a moment as he absorbed that, but then he asked, "So Coop... Her interactions with people are..."

The sun was just beginning to pop up over the horizon, its orange haze bringing with it a new day. "Strange? Matter-of-fact? Emotionless?"

"I'm not sure what adjectives I'd use to describe her, but those work in a pinch. Don't get me wrong, I love her, I just noticed she socializes differently."

"Coop isn't used to interacting with people on a daily basis. You can't tell by her face or even her words, but she truly loves it. She doesn't always understand the basic rules of society, or a metaphor, or even most common courtesies, but she tries like the dickens. I don't know how she ended up so kind when her creation was intended for evil, but she has a heart of gold—even if she can't smile very well."

Higgs gave me an odd look, his eyebrow raised. "Her creation was intended for evil?"

I patted his leg in sympathy. "I'll let *her* tell you her

origin story. It's hers to tell. I know this is a lot to consume, but do it in small doses or I can't promise you won't have nightmares."

"You're probably right. Speaking of origin stories, I got a text from Tansy while you were in getting stitched up."

"And?"

"First, she said to tell you Emile confessed to every last bit. The police and forensics are over at his apartment now, collecting the evidence… "

"You mean body parts, right? Like heads?"

"I was trying to be delicate, but yes. Also, she said to tell Mike Tyson to take a couple of days off."

I choked on a laugh as I sipped my coffee. "Do you think she fell for Coop's story about me taking Krav Maga? It's not exactly the kind of sport that would leave Emile in the shape I left him in."

Now Higgs laughed, draping his arm over my shoulders. "I think she just thinks you guys went a few rounds before we got there, and seeing as you have plenty of bruises and stitches yourself, at least as many as he does, she probably won't question it much."

I wasn't so sure. "But he was nearly catatonic, Higgs. Surely he'll tell them what I did to him."

Apparently, according to Coop, I'd really lost my ever-lovin' mind on Emile. I remembered nothing of it, but after Coop and Higgs managed to get out of the duct tape and restraints Emile had tied them up with, they'd found me throwing him around like a rag doll.

I wanted to feel a certain amount of shame at my violence, but I couldn't summon much. He'd killed Sister

Ophelia, and that hadn't even been the beginning of his long history of murder.

Higgs took a swig of coffee and nodded. "I'm sure he will, but we'll be there to back up *your* story. Don't worry. We've got it all worked out."

Folding my hands around the Styrofoam cup, I looked down at my torn-up knuckles. "Is Father Rico okay?"

"Well, he's in a lot of shock, for sure. But he didn't see Coop work her magic, if that's what you're worried about. He passed out."

"Bet you wish *you'd* passed out, huh?" I teased.

"Are you kidding me? And miss Coop literally shredding three-inch-thick rope with nothing more than a shrug of her arms? No, ma'am. I can look back on it fondly now that I'm past the freak-out stage. Don't take the coolness away from me."

I chuckled and shifted my sore foot. I'd taken some Aleve but refused the pain meds, and I was beginning to regret that choice.

"And Sister Patricia? Any news on her release?"

"She's been released from custody, free and clear. Father Rico and Deacon Cameron went to get her."

I felt sad for what she'd lose because of her affair, but maybe she'd land on her feet the way I had. I hoped for that. "She must be so upset. She's got a lot to figure out now."

"That she does, but Father Rico was ready to hear what she had to say. As to Mrs. Coletti, she could be charged with obstruction of justice for lying about that phone call between Sister P and Horatio."

Sighing, I looked off into the distance. "What a mess. I bet Mr. Coletti's going to eat Mrs. Coletti alive for that—

forget what *he* did. An affair is one thing. An accusation of murder is quite another. I feel so badly for Daniel."

"Oh, that's probably already in the works, according to Tansy. She was in the middle of questioning Mrs. Coletti again when word came in about Emile. She released Mr. Coletti and Mrs. Coletti at about the same time. So…"

I winced, imagining that mess. "I'm surprised I didn't hear the screaming all the way in the ER." I paused for a moment, still worried about Daniel. "Do you think Daniel's going to be all right, Higgs?"

"I told Tansy your concerns about him, and she's sending a social worker to take a hard look at the Colettis."

My heart shifted in my chest. "You really are a knight in shining armor, Higgs. *Thank you.*"

"You're most welcome. Hey, do you ever plan to tell Knuckles and Goose?"

I certainly wanted to, but what if they couldn't be as accepting of my condition as Higgs? I don't know that I could stand that kind of hurt and rejection.

So I simply shrugged. "I don't know. I don't want to risk our friendship. I love them like family…"

He smiled at me. "I get it, Trixie. I really do, but I want you to consider giving them more credit than that. But think it over. It's still too new. One confession at a time, yes?"

His words gave me great hope. It would be a relief if the guys knew, but I worried it could be a burden, too. For now, I had to leave this topic alone. The time would come to sort through it later when I'd slept and eaten.

"So…we have our work cut out for us when you're all healed up, yes?"

I turned in my seat to look at him, confused. "Our work cut out for us? What do you mean?"

He smiled at me, the flash of his white teeth appearing even whiter in the coming daylight. "The work where I help you figure out who this Artur is. I'm an ex-cop, Sister Trixie Lavender. It's sort of what I used to do. If we do it together, who knows what we'll be able to accomplish?"

My toes curled—well, five of them did. The other five couldn't feel anything. But more importantly, my heart curled with warmth and happiness. "You do realize, I didn't really figure out this murder. In fact, I don't figure them out at all. It all usually falls into my lap when I'm in the middle of fighting for my life at the hands of a killer."

"Well, you *did* figure it out, it was just poor timing. But it doesn't matter. We can still try. Coop said you don't know anything about this demon. So let's find something out."

My heart sped up as he looked at me. "You really want to help me, Higgs?"

Leaning toward me, his eyes grew soft. "I admit I was a little taken aback at first. I mean, it's like an episode of *Supernatural* and I'm sorry if that upset you. But I'm past that now. So yes, of course I want to help you, Trixie. I'll always want to help you. I'll always want to be a lot of things for you—*with* you. Being a part of your life is one of those things. If Artur is a part of you and your life, let's figure out what we can do to manage him or whatever needs doing."

Reaching up, I cupped his face with my bruised hand, still astounded. My eyes filled with tears. "*Really?*"

"Really," he rumbled, the sound coming from somewhere deep in his chest.

And then he leaned in and kissed me.

I didn't have much time to dwell on all the things that kiss did to my insides, because Coop pulled up then, and Knuckles and Goose piled out of the car with their arms wide open, their faces full of worry.

"Trixie girl! Oh, you poor baby," Knuckles cooed as he rushed toward me and scooped me up in a gentle hug.

Goose was right behind him, pushing Higgs out of the way to cup my cheek. "Kiddo, what the heck are we gonna do with you? What is it about you and a good knock-down drag-out? C'mon, little lady. Let's get you home so we can fix you right up. Knuckles has some breakfast just waitin' in the oven that needs eatin'."

"You guys! What are you doing here? You should both still be asleep," I chastised, even if I loved the effort they'd made.

"You don't think either one of us could sleep after hearing what happened to you, do you, Trix? Not a chance. So I got up and cooked and baked and Goose drove me crazy with the Home Shopping Network."

I laughed as they settled me into our beat-up Caddy, tucking a blanket around me, gently kissing my cheek. And as always, my heart overflowed with love for these people I'd come to consider family.

Higgs climbed in beside me and reached for my hand, and all the feelings I'd felt when he'd kissed me came rushing back. I wanted time to process those emotions, but Knuckles looked over the seat at me and grinned. "You ready for the best egg and spinach frittata of your life, kiddo?"

"I'm always ready for anything I didn't make," I said with a grin, letting my head fall to the seat.

"Then home, James!" Knuckles called out and tweaked Coop's cheek.

She swatted at him with her free hand and frowned. "My name isn't James, Knuckles. It's Cooper O'Shea."

As everyone laughed at Coop's protest, I snuggled down under the blanket and let myself relive that kiss.

And then I smiled…and I didn't stop for a long time to come.

The End

(Thank you so much for grabbing a copy of *The Smoking Nun!* I hope you enjoyed and you'll come back for more adventures with Trixie, Coop and gang in *Carry On My Wayward Nun*—coming soon!)

PREVIEW ANOTHER BOOK BY DAKOTA
CASSIDY

Chapter 1

"Left, Stevie! Left!" my familiar, Belfry, bellowed, flapping his teeny bat wings in a rhythmic whir against the lash of wind and rain. "No, your other left! If you don't get this right sometime soon, we're gonna end up resurrecting the entire population of hell!"

I repositioned him in the air, moving my hand to the left, my fingers and arms aching as the icy rains of Seattle in February battered my face and my last clean outfit. "Are you sure it was *here* that the voice led you? Like right in this spot? Why would a ghost choose a cliff on a hill in the middle of Ebenezer Falls as a place to strike up a conversation?"

"Stevie Cartwright, in your former witch life, did the ghosts you once spent more time with than the living always choose convenient locales to do their talking? As I recall, that loose screw Ferdinand Santos decided to make an appearance at the gynecologist. Remember? It was all stirrups and forceps and gabbing about you going to his wife to tell her where he hid the toenail clippers. That's only one example. Shall I list more?"

Sometimes, in my former life as a witch, those who'd gone to the Great Beyond contacted me to help them settle up a score, or reveal information they took to the grave but felt guilty about taking. Some scores and guilty consciences were worthier than others.

"Fine. Let's forget about convenience and settle for getting the job done because it's forty degrees and dropping, you're going to catch your death, and I can't spend all day on a rainy cliff just because you're sure someone is trying to contact me using *you* as my conduit. You aren't like rabbit ears on a TV, buddy. And let's not forget the fact that we're unemployed, if you'll recall. We need a job, Belfry. We need big, big job before my savings turns to ashes and joins the pile that was once known as my life."

"Higher!" he demanded. Then he asked, "Speaking of ashes, on a scale of one to ten, how much do you hate Baba Yaga today? You know, now that we're a month into this witchless gig?"

Losing my witch powers was a sore subject I tried in quiet desperation to keep on the inside.

I puffed an icy breath from my lips, creating a spray from the rain splashing into my mouth. "I don't hate Baba," I replied easily.

Almost too easily.

The answer had become second nature. I responded the same way every time anyone asked when referring to the witch community's fearless, ageless leader, Baba Yaga, who'd shunned me right out of my former life in Paris, Texas, and back to my roots in a suburb of Seattle.

I won't lie. That had been the single most painful moment of my life. I didn't think anything could top being left at the altar by Warren the Wayward Warlock. Forget losing a fiancé. I had the witch literally slapped right out of me. I lost my entire being. Everything I've ever known.

Belfry made his wings flap harder and tipped his head to the right, pushing his tiny skull into the wind. "But you no likey. Baba booted you out of Paris, Stevie. Shunned you like you'd never even existed."

Paris was the place to be for a witch if living out loud was your thing. There was no hiding your magic, no fear of a human uprising or being burned at the stake out of paranoia. Everyone in the small town of Paris was paranormal, though primarily it was made up of my own kind.

Some witches are just as happy living where humans are the majority of the population. They don't mind keeping their powers a secret, but I came to love carrying around my wand in my back pocket just as naturally as I'd carry my lipstick in my purse.

I really loved the freedom to practice white magic anywhere I wanted within the confines of Paris and its rules, even if I didn't love feeling like I lived two feet from the fiery jaws of Satan.

But Belfry had taken my ousting from the witch community much harder than me—or maybe I should say he's more vocal about it than me.

So I had to ask. "Do you keep bringing up my universal shunning to poke at me, because you get a kick out of seeing my eyes at their puffiest after a good, hard cry? Or do you ask to test the waters because there's some witch event Baba's hosting that you want to go to with all your little familiar friends and you know the subject is a sore one for me this early in the 'Stevie isn't a witch anymore' game?"

Belfry's small body trembled. "You hurt my soul, Cruel One. I would never tease about something so delicate. It's neither. As your familiar, it's my job to know where your emotions rank. I can't read you like I used to because—"

"Because I'm not on the same wavelength as you. Our connection is weak and my witchy aura is fading. Yadda, yadda, yadda. I get it. Listen, Bel, I don't hate BY. She's a good leader. On the other hand, I'm not inviting her over for girls' night and braiding her hair either. She did what she had to in accordance with the white witch way. I also get that. She's the head witch in charge and it's her duty to protect the community."

"Protect-schmotect. She was over you like a champion hurdler. In a half second flat."

Belfry was bitter-schmitter.

"Things have been dicey in Paris as of late, with a lot of change going on. You know that as well as I do. I just happened to be unlucky enough to be the proverbial straw to break Baba's camel back. She made me the example to show everyone how she protects us...er, *them*. So could we not talk about her or my defunct powers or my old life anymore? Because if we don't look to the future and get me employed, we're going to have to make curtains out of your tiny wings to cover the window of our box under the bridge."

"Wait! There he is! Hold steady, Stevie!" he yelled into the wind.

We were out on this cliff in the town I'd grown up in because Belfry claimed someone from the afterlife—someone British—was trying to contact me, and as he followed the voice, it was clearest here. In the freezing rain...

Also in my former life, from time to time, I'd helped those who'd passed on solve a mystery. Now that I was unavailable for comment, they tried reaching me via Belfry.

The connection was always hazy and muddled, it came and went, broken and spotty, but Belfry wasn't ready to let go of our former life. So more often than not, over the last month since I'd been booted from the community, as the afterlife grew anxious about my vacancy, the dearly departed sought any means to connect with me.

Belfry was the most recent "any means."

"Madam *Who*?" Belfry squeaked in his munchkin voice, startling me. "Listen up, matey, when you contact a medium, you gotta turn up the volume!"

"Belfryyy!" I yelled when a strong wind picked up, lashing at my face and making my eyes tear. "This is moving toward ridiculous. Just tell whoever it is that I can't come to the phone right now due to poverty!"

He shrugged me off with an impatient flap of his wings. "Wait! Just one more sec—what's that? *Zoltar?* What in all the bloomin' afterlife is a Zoltar?" Belfry paused and, I'd bet, held his breath while he waited for an answer—and then he let out a long, exasperated squeal of frustration before his tiny body went limp.

Which panicked me. Belfry was prone to drama-ish tendencies at the best of times, but the effort he was putting into being my conduit of sorts had been taking a toll. He was all I had, my last connection to anything supernatural. I couldn't bear losing him.

So I yanked him to my chest and tucked him into my soaking-wet sweater as I made a break for the hotel we were a week from being evicted right out of.

"Belfry!" I clung to his tiny body, rubbing my thumbs over the backs of his wings.

Belfry is a cotton ball bat. He's two inches from wing to wing of pure white bigmouth and minute yellow ears and snout, with origins stemming from Honduras, Nicaragua, and Costa Rica, where it's warm and humid.

Since we'd moved here to Seattle from the blazing-hot sun of Paris, Texas, he'd struggled with the cooler weather.

I was always finding ways to keep him warm, and now that he'd taxed himself by staying too long in the crappy weather we were having, plus using all his familiar energy to figure out who was trying to contact me, his wee self had gone into overload.

I reached for the credit card key to our hotel room in my skirt pocket and swiped it, my hands shaking. Slamming the door shut with the heel of my foot, I ran to the bathroom, flipped on the lights and set Belfry on a fresh white towel. His tiny body curled inward, leaving his wings tucked under him as pinhead-sized drops of water dripped on the towel.

Grabbing the blow dryer on the wall, I turned the setting to low and began swishing it over him from a safe distance so as not to knock him off the vanity top. "Belfry! Don't you poop on me now, buddy. I need you!" Using my index and my thumb, I rubbed along his rounded back, willing warmth into him.

"To the right," he ordered.

My fingers stiffened as my eyes narrowed, but I kept rubbing just in case.

He groaned. "Ahh, yeah. Riiight there."

"Belfry?"

"Yes, Wicked One?"

"Not the time to test my devotion."

"Are you fragile?"

"I wouldn't use the word fragile. But I would use mildly agitated and maybe even raw. If you're just joking around, knock it off. I've had all I can take in the way of shocks and upset this month."

He used his wings to push upward to stare at me with his melty chocolate eyes. "I wasn't testing your devotion. I was just depleted. Whoever this guy is, trying to get you on the line, he's determined. How did you manage to keep your fresh, dewy appearance with all that squawking in your ears all the time?"

I shrugged my shoulders and avoided my reflection in the mirror over the vanity. I didn't look so fresh and dewy anymore, and I knew it. I looked tired and devoid of interest in most everything around me. The bags under my eyes announced it to the world.

"We need to find a job, Belfry. We have exactly a week before my savings account is on E."

"So no lavish spending. Does that mean I'm stuck with the very average Granny Smith for dinner versus, say, a yummy pomegranate?"

I chuckled because I couldn't help it. I knew my laughter egged him on, but he was the reason I still got up every morning. Not that I'd ever tell him as much.

I reached for another towel and dried my hair, hoping it

wouldn't frizz. "You get whatever is on the discount rack, buddy. Which should be incentive enough for you to help me find a job, lest you forgot how ripe those discounted bananas from the whole foods store really were."

"Bleh. Okay. Job. Onward ho. Got any leads?"

"The pharmacy in the center of town is looking for a cashier. It won't get us a cute house at the end of a cul-de-sac, but it'll pay for a decent enough studio. Do you want to come with or stay here and rest your weary wings?"

"Where you go, I go. I'm the tuna to your mayo."

"You have to stay in my purse, Belfry," I warned, scooping him up with two fingers to bring him to the closet with me to help me choose an outfit. "You can't wander out like you did at the farmers' market. I thought that jelly vendor was going to faint. This isn't Paris anymore. No one knows I'm a witch—" I sighed. "*Was* a witch, and no one especially knows you're a talking bat. Seattle is eclectic and all about the freedom to be you, but they haven't graduated to letting ex-witches leash their chatty bats outside of restaurants just yet."

"I got carried away: I heard 'mango chutney' and lost my teensy mind. I promise to stay in the dark hovel you call a purse—even if the British guy contacts me again."

"Forget the British guy and help me decide. Red Anne Klein skirt and matching jacket, or the less formal Blue Fly jeans and Gucci silk shirt in teal."

"You're not interviewing with Karl Lagerfeld. You're interviewing to sling sundries. Gum, potato chips, *People* magazine, maybe the occasional script for Viagra."

"It's an organic pharmacy right in that kitschy little knoll in town where all the food trucks and tattoo shops are. I'm not sure they make all-natural Viagra, but you sure sound disappointed we might have a roof over our heads."

"I'm disappointed you probably won't be wearing all those cute vintage clothes you're always buying at the thrift store if you work in a pharmacy."

"I haven't gotten the job yet, and if I do, I guess I'll just be the cutest cashier ever."

I decided on the Ann Klein. It never hurt to bring a touch of understated class, especially when the class had only cost me a total of twelve dollars.

As I laid out my wet clothes to dry on the tub and went about the business of putting on my best interview facade, I tried not to think about Belfry's broken communication with the British guy. There were times as a witch when I'd toiled over the souls who needed closure, sometimes to my detriment.

But I couldn't waste energy fretting over what I couldn't fix. And if British Guy was hoping I could help him now, he was sorely misinformed.

Maybe the next time Belfry had an otherworldly connection, I'd ask him to put everyone in the afterlife on notice that Stevie Louise Cartwright was out of order.

Grabbing my purse from the hook on the back of the bathroom door, I smoothed my hands over my skirt and squared my shoulders.

"You ready, Belfry?"

"As I'll ever be."

"Ready, set, job!"

As I grabbed my raincoat and tucked Belfry into my purse, I sent up a silent prayer to the universe that my unemployed days were numbered.

NOTE FROM DAKOTA

I do hope you enjoyed this book, I'd so appreciate it if you'd help others enjoy it, too.

Recommend it. Please help other readers find this book by recommending it.

Review it. Please tell other readers why you liked this book by reviewing it at online retailers or your blog. Reader reviews help my books continue to be valued by distributors/resellers. I adore each and every reader who takes the time to write one!

If you love the book or leave a review, please email **dakota@dakotacassidy.com** so I can thank you with a personal email. Your support means more than you'll ever know! Thank you!

ABOUT THE AUTHOR

Dakota Cassidy is a USA Today bestselling author with over thirty books. She writes laugh-out-loud cozy mysteries, romantic comedy, grab-some-ice erotic romance, hot and sexy alpha males, paranormal shifters, contemporary kick-ass women, and more.

Dakota was invited by Bravo TV to be the Bravoholic for a week, wherein she snarked the hell out of all the reality Bravo shows. She received a starred review from Publishers Weekly for Talk Dirty to Me, won a Romantic Times Reviewers' Choice Award for Kiss and Hell, along with many review site recommended reads and reviewer top pick awards.

Dakota lives in the gorgeous state of Oregon with her real-life hero and her dogs, and she loves hearing from readers!

Visit Dakota's website at http://www.dakotacassidy.com for more information.

Lemon Layne Mystery Series, a Contemporary Cozy Mystery Series

1. Prawn of the Dead
2. Play That Funky Music White Koi

Witchless In Seattle Mystery Series, a Paranormal Cozy Mystery

1. Witch Slapped
2. Quit Your Witchin'
3. Dewitched
4. The Old Witcheroo
5. How the Witch Stole Christmas
6. Ain't Love a Witch
7. Good Witch Hunting
8. Witch Way Did He Go?

Nun of Your Business Mysteries Series, a Paranormal Cozy Mystery

1. Then There Were Nun
2. Hit and Nun
3. House of the Rising Nun

Wolf Mates Series, a Paranormal Romantic Comedy

1. An American Werewolf In Hoboken
2. What's New, Pussycat?
3. Gotta Have Faith
4. Moves Like Jagger
5. Bad Case of Loving You

A Paris, Texas Romance Series, a Paranormal Romantic Comedy

1. Witched At Birth
2. What Not to Were
3. Witch Is the New Black
4. White Witchmas

Non-Series

Whose Bride Is She Anyway?

Polanski Brothers: Home of Eternal Rest

Sexy Lips 66

Accidentally Paranormal Series, a Paranormal Romantic Comedy

Interview With an Accidental—a free introductory guide to the girls of the Accidentals!

1. The Accidental Werewolf
2. Accidentally Dead
3. The Accidental Human
4. Accidentally Demonic
5. Accidentally Catty
6. Accidentally Dead, Again
7. The Accidental Genie
8. The Accidental Werewolf 2: Something About Harry

9. The Accidental Dragon

10. Accidentally Aphrodite

11. Accidentally Ever After

12. Bearly Accidental

13. How Nina Got Her Fang Back

14. The Accidental Familiar

15. Then Came Wanda

16. The Accidental Mermaid

17. Marty's Horrible, Terrible, Very Bad Day

The Hell Series, a Paranormal Romantic Comedy

1. Kiss and Hell

2. My Way to Hell

The Plum Orchard Series, a Contemporary Romantic Comedy

1. Talk This Way

2. Talk Dirty to Me

3. Something to Talk About

4. Talking After Midnight

The Ex-Trophy Wives Series, a Contemporary Romantic Comedy series

1. You Dropped a Blonde On Me

2. Burning Down the Spouse

3. Waltz This Way

The Fangs of Anarchy Series, a Paranormal Urban Fantasy

1. Forbidden Alpha

2. Outlaw Alpha

Made in the USA
Columbia, SC
19 July 2019